A MARIJUANA MAN

A DEALER'S DIARY

STEVE KRAVETZ

ISBN: 978-0-9996355-0-6

Published by: Steve Kravetz with the full support of the Brotherhood of Smoke.

Cover design: Steve Kravetz // Artwork by: jbinspiration@fiverr

Icon character design: Steve Kravetz//Artwork by: jonathanshih@fiverr

This book is dedicated to two special women in my life.

Ann Kravetz, my mom, always wanted me to follow my dreams and encouraged my creative side.

Darlene Harris-Kravetz, my beloved mate for almost 30 years. I can hear her now, "Steve this book is our past and our future." We had lived those years firsthand, she especially. Graduating from the University of California at Berkley in the 60's, she was in Chicago in 1968 for the demonstrations at the National Democratic convention, the following year she was arrested at the peace protest at the Lincoln Memorial in Washington DC. One of her last requests was for me to finish this project, which started in 1983 as an idea. In 2010 it first became a word on paper. Today is its birth.

Thank you, ladies

Contributors:

There have been a few people who also gave me impute and their important time.

My Dad Lew Kravetz who as of today is 99 years young and walks proudly without a cane or walker, he gave me tenacity and his limitless love.

My Nephew Lee Daniel Kravetz, who gave me his impute and direction from the start.

My old English professor and longtime friend **Dr. James Baird** who shared those turbulent years with us and gave me his expertise on this work.

My new friend Arthur Wyckoff gave me directions for the publishing of this book.

My classmate Ms. Marty McCaffrey Jackson put the final spit polish on this story.

To the few friends and family who have endured my obsession with this book.

Lastly to all the **real smugglers** who took the risk of succeeding or failing, who without them we would have no smoke or story.

Thank you all

PREFACE

A Marijuana Man is a fictional story characterizing the life and times of an ambitious man from 1966 through 1983. This not anyone's personal story and this book is not meant to be used as a "How to..." textbook or to glorify the drug business. It is the enactment of the times and how one man conducted himself while doing his business and living life during these times. It also reflects the period where the major historical events of this time were to be the catalysts for the "hippie" generation and the metamorphosis of America.

I hope you enjoy the story. So, find yourself a comfortable place to sit or lie, burn one if you want, and take this trip and travel back in time, with me.

HISTORICAL TRUTHS

On December 3, 2008, a group of archaeologists working in Northwest China discovered a 2,700-year-old tomb; inside, the preserved body of a man and all his most precious items. Among his possessions was an old leather pouch containing herbs and roots, but also the flower buds from the cannabis plant. This is not the first tomb found to have safe-guarded ancient smoking hemp, but it is the oldest. Now we have proof that for at least 2,700 years, men have used this plant to intoxicate themselves, their friends and guest for entertainment and social interactions and to begin the **Brotherhood of Smoke.**

THE PRESENT: 1984

There is nothing like the clanging of steel prison doors against their iron frames to jar you into reality. I am a federal prisoner, number S.T. 83-7964-976. For the next seven years I will reside in the federal prison at Seagoville, Texas, or anyplace else the United States Federal prison system wishes for me to occupy space. My current elegant accommodation with gourmet meals and glamorous attire is not what this story is really about though.

My present situation is not the beginning of this story but rather the end of a story that began almost eighteen years ago when I was just another dumb teenager who knew *everything* and had life all figured out. My fondest memories were of my maternal grandfather or Zady to me, a small man who had come to the U.S. as a young husband from Belarus, Russia, at the turn of the century like so many Jews running from the Pogroms. He was a master Tailor by trade, working the fabric to his will and me too, his youngest grandson. Our conversations were not equal exchanges, but more like educational wisdom delivered by Zady via philosophical analogies in Yiddish and then again in English. He would advise me**, "What you don't see with your eyes, don't invent with your mouth."** And my favorite maxim, **"A Jew is 28% *fear*, 2% *sugar* and 70% *chutzpah*."** In light of all that has happened, I can hear him admonishing me from his grave, "***Max* you should have used your *Kop* (Head) not your *Tuchas* (Butt),"** and then the zinger, **"*Experience is what we call the *accumulation of our mistakes*."** They are **Zadyism.**

A Zadyism is a piece of knowledge distributed verbally with love, and insightful knowledge of life. Some of these bits of knowledge are original, but most are borrowed/stolen from someone else (though he never claimed any of them as his original thoughts, "*just good words.*")

My name is Max Gold. In the late summer of 1966 after I had graduated from high school in Dallas, my best friend Rodger Sampson and I, had planned a road trip to Austin, just 190 miles south, down I-35 as our last hoorah before our college classes started at North Texas State University in Denton.

Austin had a great growing music scene, which we both loved. I was not quite six feet tall and a wiry one hundred sixty-eight pounds. I had shoulder length, reddish brown hair, almost black eyes and a rich tan complexion year-round. My nose is larger than an average Catholic school kid, but smaller than some of my fellow Jewish friends. I also had an adventurous spirit and loved a challenge. I had grown up in a typical middle-class family. My dad Harold Gold had met my mom Miriam at a USO dance in New York City before he was shipped out to Europe to defend our country during World War ll. I have an older sister, Judy Gold Blumberg, who was born in 1945 and is now married to Dr. Joel Blumberg. Danny, my older brother, was born in 1946, and was now attending the University of Texas, in Austin, and then there was me, the baby, in 1948.

Rodger had been my best friend since third grade, his mom a nurse, and dad a Master Sergeant recruiter with the Army, had lived just two doors down from mine for many years. Even though he was two years older than me, Rodger had been held back in first grade, so he was only one grade ahead of me in school. At 6'2" Rodger is much taller than me and weighs close to two hundred and 225 pounds. Rodger is shaped like an upside-down pear, broad at the shoulders and small at the hips. He has dark blond hair and most intense blue eyes. He is what my mom would call "movie-star" handsome. As Roger will tell it," I may not be the smartest guy in the room, but I am the most charming." He's just a big lapdog.

3 |

Friends for life, we complement each other. I could get wild hair and he would calm me down, so I could reconsider the bad decision I was about to make. I was the natural leader, Rodger the happy, fun, agreeable co-pilot.

Enterprisers even as young kids, Rodger and I collected empty drink bottles to return to the store for two cents cash each. One time, while exploring on our bikes, we came across a burned-out house. Inside we found lots of burnt wood, furniture, and trash, but it also had over 150 pounds of copper wire and pipes lying between the walls and floors, which for a week, we cut and hauled out on our bikes. It brought us $47.50, our first big job together. Though it was dirty and smelly work, it was also exciting and dangerous. Are these burnt wires I am about to touch still carrying live electricity? Will the floor hold me or is it too burned out? I guess we relished the thrill.

We also got into all kinds of trouble together as teenagers. Like the time just after Spring Break in 63, we locked three live chickens, one a rooster, in the school's public-address broadcasting room. Leaving the mic open and locking the door, Rodger pocketed the only key. When school resumed after the break, the entire student body and faculty were greeted by the rooster crowing with the hens clucking in the background. That one cost us one month of detention after school but was worth it as that caper became a legend at the school. There is still a small golden rooster in the school's trophy case to this day.

My dad and Rodger's used to play golf together on Sunday mornings, rain or shine. Rodger and I one time, bought some trick golf balls, one that did crazy turns, one that would hardly roll at all. After we exchanged our new balls for the ones in their golf bags. I had forgotten all about them, at least until the next Sunday afternoon. Harold and Mr. Sampson were pissed. They had been playing doubles against friends at $ 10 a hole. The ball they got out of their bags had magnets in them, so they would stick on the lip of the cups, not go in but would hang on the lip. Harold did not think it was as funny as I did, and Rodger's father was a real hard ass, so we found ourselves climbing ladders, removing the screens and washing all the window of both of the houses, and ours was a two- story. So that adventure, as window washers, was not as fun or profitable.

Our carefree days seemed to end abruptly on the day President John F Kennedy was assassinated here in Dallas November 22, 1963, and on the very same day halfway around the world Rodger's father was assassinated by an unidentified enemy in a place called Vietnam. The family never got straight answers from the government about the details of Robert Sampson's death, just a standard Western Union telegram and that simply read.

THE SECRETARY OF THE ARMY ASKED ME TO EXPRESS HIS DEEP REGRET THAT

YOU'RE HUSBAND, MASTER SERGEANT ROBERT SAMP-SON, DIED IN VIETNAM

ON 22 NOVEMBER 1963, FROM WOUNDS RECEIVED WHILE ON COMBAT OPERATION

WHEN HIT BY

HOSTILE ARMS FIRE

PLEASE ACCEPT MY DEEPEST SYMPATHY. THIS CONFIRMS PERSONAL

NOTIFICATION

MADE BY A REPRESENTATIVE OF THE SECRETARY OF THE ARMY.

Arthur R, Pardham Major General United State Army: Adjunct General

That was the day happy-go- lucky Rodger began to change. He became almost obsessed with what would become a major weakness, women. Like a kid in a candy store, he wanted to taste each and because of his looks and charm, the ladies loved him back. Shortly after the new year of 1965, Rodger and his mom moved to Denton for her new job as an emergency room head nurse at the county hospital. Rodger had just graduated high school and then he received a change in his draft status to 1-A. A week later he registered for a minimum 12 hours at NTSU to keep the draft board off his back, at least until he could get a permanent exemption from the draft board. Rodger was the sole surviving male of the Sampson family, and it would change his draft status permanently.

To help his mom financially Rodger worked at a man's clothing store off the downtown square for as many hours as he could manage.

This trip in 66 was long overdue and well planned out clothes, check. Cash, check, gas in car, check, directions, check, check. We knew the distance from Dallas to Austin necessitated an overnight stay either at Danny's apartment or my cousin Bobby's house. Bobby was a couple of years older than Danny and had already graduated from the University of Texas. Bobby had stayed in Austin, manages and bartending at a bar downtown.

Once we arrived in Austin, Rodger and I met Danny for dinner at the Night Bird, a restaurant just off campus. My brother is a genius when it comes to electronics. He's the guy Heath Electronics stores were open for, which also happens to be where Danny worked and co-managed. After dinner he went home with the care packages that Mom had sent while Rodger and I headed to 6th Street in an area where there were lots of small bars and clubs.

Over the next few hours, we bar hopped, had a few beers while enjoying country music and some jazz. We caught Muddy Waters, the Delta Blue guitarist and singer performing at The Old Rusty Door. He played two of my favorites "(*I'm Your*) *Hoochie-Coochie Man*" and "*I Can't Be Satisfied.*" At close to midnight, we headed to my Cousin Bobby's workplace.

"Do you guys have I.D.s?" Bob asked as he smiled and pulled us the last draw for the night. After helping him to close up, we followed him in his Datsun to the small frame two-bedroom bungalow in East Austin where he lived with Butch, his German shepherd and Cindy, his lady.

"I have not been home very long myself," Cindy said, shortly after we arrived that night. "I worked a late shift at the hospital, but I did get a chance to sneak downstairs to visit Gail for a few minutes"

Bobby turned to us. "You guys heard about that crazy ex-Marine Charles Whitman, right? He's the guy who shot those people from the University tower a couple weeks ago That S.O.B. killed sixteen people.

Well, Cindy's friend Gail was one of the thirty- one lucky people. She caught a bullet, and it hit her inches from her heart. If she had been facing him instead of walking away, she would be dead. Fortunately, she will be getting out of the hospital soon."

"Didn't Whitman end up being killed by a group of Police officers himself?" Rodger cracked?

"Good riddance, "Cindy replied. "That crazy son of a bitch should have just killed himself in the first place if he was that unhappy. Why did he need to take it out on other people?" No arguing with that logic.

At 1:00 a.m. we all crashed. I took the couch and Rodger went to the other bedroom. I woke to the sound of bacon popping in a pan, toast springing from the toaster and eggs being whipped in a bowl. Cindy was in the kitchen making breakfast. What a great start to a new day. After breakfast, as we got ready to leave, Bobby said, "Hey you guys, I got some new records you're going to go crazy over, and there's something here you need to check out." He sat down on the couch, pulled out a lid from a shoe box that had been slid under the couch, which is why I had not noticed it before. He proceeded to make a small cigarette, or so I thought. He lit it and passed it to Cindy. They each inhaled the smoke, holding it in their lungs. The smell was like burning rope or dried cow manure.

Cindy passed the cig to Rodger, and he followed suit but let out a "Whoa" and shook his head as he blew out the foggy smoke.

Then it was my turn. "Go ahead and try this shit little Cuz,"

I did try it, but at first all I could do was choke and cough. Cindy came to my rescue, "Max, pull a little fresh air in as you suck, now hold that smoke in your lungs as long as possible".

When I took her advice, and added more fresh air to my draw, I was right on the mark. Until that day Rodger and I had consumed beer and wine and even some hard liquor, but no drugs. I had heard of marijuana, of course, but I did not know anyone who actually smoked this "wicked weed." I do know that if I had not smoked that day, one day shortly after, I would have found my way to this sweet euphoria and become a lifetime member of the **"Brotherhood of Smoke."**

The smoke went from my mouth through my lungs, then to my blood vessels and finally to my mind. I sat back, letting the grass take its effect. The music on the stereo grabbed me like nothing before. I was there with the band focusing on every chord, every riff, and every nuance of tone. The music invaded my very being, energizing all my brain cells to vibrate with every beat of the drummer. I looked over to Rodger. His eyes were shut, but his head seemed to be a musical instrument playing with the band. I had never been so relaxed yet so alive. My mind was racing with a thousand thoughts at one time. Where is this being recorded? Who is hearing this besides me? Are they as impressed with this as I am? Who else hears the little changes? And yet everything was so clear. I had consumed various liquors before, but except for beer, I really did not care for alcohol and, especially, the next-day hangovers. This was *totally* different from an alcohol buzz. I did not feel queasy or wobbly; I was not feeling pulled down, or heavy, just mellow.

As the hours passed by unnoticed, we talked and laughed until after lunch when Bobby had to go to work. Lunch was one of my greatest meals ever. The Grape Nehi exploded in my mouth, the crunchy and salty potato chips melted on my tongue, and when the peanut butter sandwich stuck to roof of my mouth, we all had a big laugh on me. Better than my mom's Sunday pot roast dinner.

Bobby said, "Let me show you guys a couple of things to make things go easier. First, pull the buds off the stem. Roll the bud with your thumb and any other finger to break the pot down into small, granular pieces. Remove these small seeds and stems. Take the rolling paper and make a V or U and hold it in one hand while you use the other to fill it up. Fold the paper over and roll. Put a little moisture on the edge, and you guys know what to do from there. Say, if you guys are interested in buying some to take home, I get it cheap by buying it by the pound, so I'll sell you guys a few lids if you want." Rodger and I each rolled a joint for the trip home and we also left with two lids, or two ounces, apiece at the cost of $8.00 for 1/8 of a pound.

This trip home was the fastest three and half hours I've ever spent coming or going anywhere.

As a happy newly inducted member of the **"Brotherhood of Smoke,"** this trek to Austin was one I would gladly make several times a month, sometimes with Rodger and sometimes soloed.

Within a week or so of our Austin trip I had moved out of my parents' home and had a new residency, a small apartment in Denton, Texas. It was, at that time, just a short forty-five-minute drive up I-35 north to North Texas State University's Denton's campus. The University required freshmen to live in a college dorm on campus, but North Texas had so many commuter students, it was hard for the college to keep up with all of us. So I took advantage of the situation to live off campus by using Rodger's mom's address as mine so that I was in compliance with the college's policy. The enrollment on campus that year was about 12,000 students, compared to the University of Texas at Austin which had a student body of over 27,000. My rent was $65 per month, all utilities included.

I was an independent guy and starting life on my own without parental or college administrative control. I was taking fifteen credit hours per week, mostly early morning classes. I liked to get up early and get my schoolwork done, so I had lots of free time. I still worked Friday afternoons and all- day Saturday at the family appliance store, making $2.00 an hour so I averaged $30.00 a week. My parents paid my rent and day-to-day expenses as they did for my brother and had for my sister when she was at school. With only my car payment of $35.00 per month as my financial obligation, I had plenty of discriminatory cash. Denton is also the home to Texas Woman's University with an enrollment of 6,000 females, so add the two universities, the supply of available women to men was seven women students for every college man in Denton. For Roger it was a smorgasbord of delights.

Most parties on and off campus had plenty of liquor. Underage drinking was the standard, not the exception, but no drugs. A typical off-campus party involved beer, or the ever- popular trash can brew, which consisted of four gallons of 180 proof Ever clear and two fifths of vodka. Then a lot of Hawaiian Punch and several large cans of fruit cocktail which were added and mixed in a new (usually) 30-gallon garbage can. Fruit will float in Hawaiian Punch, but once the liquor is added to the punch, the floating fruit sinks to the bottom of the can as it also drops to the bottom of drinking cups. This would encourage novice drinkers to empty their cups quickly to get to the sweet fruit, so that many of these party people got very drunk very fast, the plan all along.

Denton was no Music Mecca as was Austin, but the college would bring in some big-name bands. Rodger and his date had front-row seats for the Four Tops and Willie Nelson. I remember a great group who would become very big, Ike and Tina Turner and their revue. They were rocking; all the kids stood through their entire performance. The one thing North Texas State did have was a world-renowned school of jazz, which brought to the school a lot of budding musicians who also played in weekend bands.

Three weeks after school started, I made my second trip back to Austin alone. Bobby introduced me to his dealer, Rudy, a Hispanic about twenty-five and a very verbal, likeable guy. Over a shared joint I asked, "So Rudy how did you get into this business"?

"I was carrying pot in my diapers for my family since I was a week old. My family would cross at least once a day, sometimes more. I did that every day until I was three when my younger brother had diaper duty and I was promoted to carrying a backpack. Now I'm selling it to guys like you two "gringos", he laughed. "Your prices today Max is, $60 per pound of freshly delivered straight from the sunny fields of Mexico FOB/freight on board Austin Texas. I'm selling my lids for $8.00 here in Austin, and I heard some guy off the square is selling small match boxes for $ 5.00 and that includes S&S, seeds and stems. So how much you want?" I left with two pounds.

In comparison, a gallon of gas was 28 cents. A new Chevy Impala could be bought loaded for $2200 or so and, a *new* custom-built North Dallas 3200 square foot brick home on a 100 by 150- foot lot listed for $35,000. Minimum wage had just gone up to $1.25 an hour. Which meant it took six hours of most people wages to buy one ounce of cannabis.

Over the first few months I had started to turn a few new friends on to smoking pot, and the **"Brotherhood of Smoke"** expanded. Of course, they responded to the pot as I had. At first, I was giving free joints to a small group of friends. As the group grew, I found myself selling joints for $2.00 each. With a $4.00 dollar investment, I could get a $36.00 net return. And the fact that we were all breaking the law, which at that time could put us in a very dark hole called the Texas Department of Correction or TDC, for 10 years to life, just for one piece of stem or a single seed. This also added to the mystique and titillation. We were rebels, outlaws, all without getting our hands too dirty. Last but not least, we got to shoot the finger to the establishment, the "Man" and this bonus was for free as long as you did not get caught. In those early days you could trust everyone you shared smoke with, for we were all part of the conspiracy, by becoming members of **the Brotherhood**.

Even now there is something special about sitting with a group of old and new friends, passing a joint and sharing the smoke experience, becoming **"Smoke Brothers."** I do not know what our Native American brothers smoked in their pipes, but I am sure they felt the smoking and passing of the pipe was as special a social event for them and their guests as it was for us. Pipe, bong or joint, the feeling of community connection prevailed. When you get together to drink alcohol, you don't share the glass, but **the Brothers of Smoke** pass the enlightenment of the smoke, from one hand to another to another until it comes back to you, a completed circle.

From the start I was making good money, and quickly my friends started to ask to buy in ounces or lids. I was in business without really trying.

In October, Rodger finally got his exemption from the draft board, so he no longer had to worry about ending up as a combatant in Vietnam. He quit school to work full time selling women's sportswear on the road. He was making more money and meeting more women. He traveled to Texas, Oklahoma, Louisiana and Arkansas, calling on department stores and specialty shops. Selling to women was right up Rodger's alley. I saw him less but getting together was still something we did at least once a month. After Hanukah and Christmas, when Rodger came home for the holidays, we headed south in his new 1967 Chrysler 300. We were homing pigeons returning for feeding. I had cash in my pocket to spend on marijuana and music and that's all we were really looking to do for the next few days.

On this trip, we had found, as I found once before, the product had not yet arrived in Austin from wherever it had begun its journey and we had no idea how long we would have to wait. After spending the next twenty-six hours down on 6th street, or just hanging out and staying stoned, I got an idea. **"If opportunity does not knock, build a door."**

"Look, man," I said. "Let's go south to find some weed ourselves." Rodger just shrugged, so we headed south for the Mexican border. If the green did not come to us, we would go to it.

We had no plans about where to go, where to buy or how to get the cannabis back across the border even if we were lucky enough to score. I had done well enough in high school Spanish and could converse with my father's Hispanic employees easily, so I felt language would not be an issue. Rodger responded, "We don't know anyone in Mexico City or Monterrey, so it might be difficult to locate a dealer? "

"Maybe we should try a resort town because we could fit in easily and maybe meet some Mexican kids on the beach and score a connection there."

At that time the only resort town that we knew of was Acapulco, 736 miles south of Laredo, Texas. We had heard, from Rudy, that the roads in Mexico were in good shape and that the gas was cheap. We drove Rodger's new ride south with only the clothes on our backs and two sample bags full of women's clothing samples.

Laredo is 200 miles south of Austin; it is a major border-crossing town where travelers between the two countries cross the "Old Muddy" Rio Grande River into Mexico or into the United States.

We had to stop at a gas station just before we got to Laredo. While I was filling up, Rodger struck up a conversation with one of the girls filling up next to us.

"Hey, Max, listen to this. Mary here and her group just came from the border. Tell him Mary, what happened."

She had a squeaky, Minnie Mouse voice, so I almost laughed until her words grabbed my attention. "We got turned back at the International Bridge by the Mexican Border Guards."

"Why? "I asked before she could finish her sentence.

Mary looked at me with disgust, but continued, "Our boyfriends have shoulder-length hair. They told us that the Mexican government was no longer allowing long-haired males into Mexico. They do not want any dirty "hippies" to invade their county."

I apologized to Mary for laughing and thanked her for the Intel. Rodger had already gone in to play and when he came out; he had a pair of scissors wrapped in his fingers. My hair was down to my shoulders, but I usually kept it in a ponytail. Rodger's hair was medium length, just covering his ears. We took turns working on the other. "Just a light trim, if you please," I directed Rodger as he began snipping. The end result: we could easily pass for Wally and Beaver Cleaver.

The border bridge had four lanes each way and walkways for pedestrian traffic. On the American side we were waved through. On the other side, the Mexican authorities then checked our car to make sure we were not smuggling in any contraband, which really meant firearms.

If we had not stopped for gas and gotten the heads up on the new hair policy, we would have been turned away at the border.

The next 700-plus miles were through the center of Mexico. The landscape was intense, rugged, and often beautiful, much like the U.S. must have been hundreds of years ago. We saw very impoverished people living a very primitive existence mostly in mud-brick adobe homes, but some dwellings were just lean-tos with tin roofs. Not knowing any other way of life, they seemed happy, and they made the best of what they did have. The trip seemed to go forever, but we finally got to Acapulco. Upon arrival, we headed for the beautiful sugar- sand beach. The high, rugged cliffs bordering the beach ran up to the mountains in the background. We watched a couple of world-famous cliff divers plunge from the high elevated rocks into the beautiful blue waters of the Pacific Ocean for money. "Wow! Look at those guys, Rodger, you got to admire their guts.

"Yea well it's not my career choice and I am dam glad of it', besides it looks like a hard way to make a living."

Acapulco is a resort city, attracting many people from Europe, South America and the U.S.A. It had lots of hotels and cantinas, shops and restaurants up and down the strip, the main road through town. We spotted a small, less busy part of the beach between a couple of their large resort hotels. This was in an area that seemed to cater to mostly locals, so that's where we went. One problem, as we walked the beach, we noticed almost all of the peddlers on the beach selling silver jewelry, handmade pottery, puppets, or blankets were either old women or young boys, not exactly the connections I wanted to make. For whatever reason, this just did not feel right, so we chilled out at the beach to watch people. Near sunset we found ourselves in a small bar and grill on one of the side streets off the beach. We ordered ceviche, a local seafood dish of raw fish cured in lime juice, served with chili peppers and a Cerveza, Mexican beer. The food was excellent and the beers cold and cheap. The bar had a lively, loud brassy mariachi band to entertain us.

I had been conversing in Spanish with one of the barkeeps off and on for several hours. His name was Juan Schwartz, from Puerto Rico. When I asked him if he or his family was Jewish, he nodded and said, "I came here to work eight years ago from Puerto Rico and married a beautiful native woman. We live up in the mountains above the city in a type of.....commune I believe you call it." What are the chances of meeting a Sephardi Jew living and working in this town one in a million? At about 11: 00 p.m. Juan asked, "Hey, what are you guys really doing here? You don't look like tourists, and you really look out of place with your hair and everything." I explained the haircuts and told him of Rodger's coming here to sell dresses, and me just tagging along. "Maybe," he said and let it drop. Then just before closing, he leaned over the bar and asked again in a whisper, "Max what you guys really here for?" I repeated the same old story, but he just stared back at me and whispered, "Buuul

Shiiit. You guys are here to buy marijuana, am I right?" I figured it was now or never to let the beast out of the box.

"Yes, Brother, I am here to buy your green product. You got me. Can you help a fellow member of the tribe?" Before I could finish my statement, Juan was howling with laughter. The few remaining customers and staff checked us out. I just hoped I'd made a good choice in trusting him.

"What's he laughing at?" Rodger grumbled.

"Just a sec, Rodg."

"Max, listen," Juan said after he quit laughing. "I am not a marijuana dealer, but my father-in-law does sell some locally, and it helps our family and my village. Tell you what. Give me some money. I don't know what he charges, but I'll get you as much as I can for whatever you have to spend. You guys meet me here tomorrow night before I go to work, okay?" I gave Juan $400 cash in U.S. $20.00 bills. "Follow me," he said. So, we did, as we walked, I explained to Rodger what had transpired as we went down the beach to a small motel where his own family stayed when they came to visit from Puerto Rico. His last words were, "Adios," before he headed out. That much cash could keep many an area family fed for many months. I was not worried... much.

The next day was spent buying T-shirts, sunglasses and swimsuits, we were playing like typical tourists, though as the day passed, I became concerned that I might have been naïve and started to contemplate what could go wrong. Juan, a no show, Juan brings packaged weeds or worse yet, Juan could bring the police. At 6:30 and still no-Juan, I began to sweat. "Let's check out of the hotel and get something to eat. If Juan isn't back by the time we finish, we will have to deal with it." The raw fish did not seem as zesty as it had the day before. After our dinner, we went back to the car. We were discussing our next bad move when Rodger looked up.

"Max, check this out." My focus shifted to a scene from an old Hollywood western film of the '40s or '50s. There, in his entire cool, wearing a large sombrero was Juan riding a small burro. On his beast of burden were large open-woven baskets, one on each side.

"The baskets normally carry beans, or squash," Juan told Rodger and I as we were unloading the 20 kilos of gold and green marijuana into Rodger's trunk. There were forty-four pounds of very fragrant, almost to the point of intoxication, Cannabis. Twenty parcels that looked like large bricks covered in old newspaper. I was to learn later that this marijuana was known as, "Acapulco Gold." On my first deal I had hit a home run and didn't even know it yet.

After we were loaded, Juan looked up, smiled and said," Were you just a little worried or lot worried I was not coming back?" He was laughing, enjoying kidding me. He did not stick around long after that and we began our long journey north.

As we drove back to the U.S. border, we quickly realized we had to find a way to kill the smell, and more importantly, a plan on how I was going to get my treasure across the border. I knew we could not simply drive it across, and I didn't have the time or patience to try to find someone to do it for me. The only possible idea I could come up with was to take it across myself. I pondered that for quite a few miles on our journey back home. Late at night we pulled off the highway onto a dirt road, if you could call it that, to air out my stash and to see just what I had to work with.

Rodger removed the trunk lightbulb to avoid attention and we examined the load. By moonlight we stared for a while at nineteen fully wrapped packages and one broken-open brick, three canvas covering sample bags and the pair of scissors.

"Well, I could empty out one of these sample bags then hang the sample clothes on this back seat bar. These bags just pull apart like Christmas boxes." Rodger explained, "And then if you put your pot in, we close it and put the canvas cover back on. I also hope it keeps the odor down too?"

"Yeah, it will make it easier for me to carry the dead weight". After repacking the bag and hanging the dresses, we left the windows down and trunk lid up, so as to air out the insides, then we slept in the car for the next few hours. During the rest of the trip, my mind raced on the logistics of looking for a crossing, where to go to look for a crossing, and how far upriver I needed to start looking for a crossing. The more I thought about it, the more questions I had.

When we got close to the outskirts of Nuevo Laredo, Mexico, we started looking in earnest for a road that would take us even close to the Rio Grande. We spent the next ninety minutes going down road after road after road, trying to find that river. Even after we did find it, we had to find a place to get us even closer to the shoreline. Amazingly, we did not see very many people around and finally, we hit the perfect drop-off point. It was a little muddy, but not too bad. We looked around. It was very dark, quiet, not a single dog was barking. I pulled out the case and got my bearings. From studying the North Star, I figured out which way was north; then I headed down to the riverbank. At the end of December in South Texas, the weather was not freezing cold, but it was not tropically hot either, especially at night. I was wearing only my now cutoff jeans, white T-shirt, and white Converse high tops. I looked at the flowing, inky water. It looked ten miles across. "Well," I said, "it's now or never."

As I took my first couple of steps, I told Rodger, "I'll see you on the flip side." But I did not hear him drive off; I was too busy worrying about drowning. After the second step, there was no third. I was in water over my neck and moving down under. I thought, "Now I know how Pharaoh's warriors must have felt in their full body armor as the water came from all sides to pull them down into the depths of the Nile." I had forty-four pounds of green gold in my hands, and nothing was going to pry it from my grip.

The Rio Grande was a lot colder than I expected and it had a putrid smell. I'm thinking, "What the hell were you thinking, Max? My fate was in a case full of marijuana. To my utter amazement it began to float. "Thank you, God," came from my lips even before I took the first kick of freedom. Zady always would say that **"God watches over fools."** thankfully! I had always been a strong swimmer, but the water's temperature was beginning to pull at my strength, causing the next round of fear. I started to kick more vigorously and had slowly made some progress, yet a third set of fears came to me. How far upriver am I? Can I make it to the other side before I cross under the International Bridge? I had visions of the *Dallas Morning News* headlines reading, "Area student caught floating large quantity of illegal marijuana across the Mexican border." All I could realistically do was kick and kick and kick some more while my mind dealt with all the demons that taunted me as I floated and kicked. I was egging myself on as well. Finally, I felt the bottom of the river on my knees. I was exhausted, cold and had no idea where I was. I crawled up the riverbank listening to my heart beating like crazy from the adrenaline. My teeth were chattering like I was a squirrel eating a nut and I felt every muscle in my body screaming from extreme exertion. What I had just done finally hit me, "Max, you son of a bitch, you did it!"

I don't remember how or what I did for the next few hours, except that I moved through thick, thorny brush and trees. I pulled that case as if my mind, body and spirit had melted. Eventually, after what seemed like days, I saw a small light off in the distance. I finally got closer and then stashed the case under the old mesquite tree's dark, hard- textured, thorny limb. I walked up to what was a small two-pump gas station. In front, patiently waiting for customers, sat an old Hispanic lady on a well-worn, chrome-framed, vinyl-covered kitchen chair from the '50s. I am sure I must've been a strange sight to her; a wet, skinny Anglo coming out of the woods in the middle of the night. She just looked up at me and said nothing, as if I was just one of many who passed here, going somewhere else. I asked in Spanish," Podria yo tenga a mano un vaso de agua"? She gracefully got up and then returned with a clean glass of water. "Mucho gracias," I said as I reached for the glass and asked for directions to I-35. I gave her back the empty glass and thanked her once more. She never said a word to me the whole time and only pointed toward the road in front to direct me where I should go. I went back to my cache and headed down the white rock road toward the interstate. After a while, I sat down on my case to take a break. Looking up I could see the millions of stars that lit the dark sky because no lights from a city penetrated this area. I was floating on adrenaline high and pumped. Everything seemed amazing to me at that particular moment, a feeling I will never forget. Joy in its purest form spread through me, I was on such a natural high that most people could never imagine or will ever experience. I was for the first time, one with the universe.

I had been sitting on the case for no more than ten minutes on Interstate 35 heading north about eight miles south of the State Highway 83 cut off to Chrystal City when who should show up? Honest to God Rodger. I could not have planned it better if we actually knew what we were doing.

Rodger's story was equally bizarre. "Max, when I left you at the river, I tried to find my way back to the border, but I found myself lost in the backroads. I eventually found my way back to the International Bridge and crossed through Mexican customs with no problems. The U.S. border access was a different story. I had not been waiting in line very long when an agent approached my car."

Rodger described him as a character out of a movie script." He was a large man who was wearing dark glasses even though it was nighttime and wore a hat in the style of a Marine drill sergeant. The officer leans into my window, and with a stern, forceful voice asked me, "Where you been, boy?"

Rodger told me, "I was a bit nervous, but replied, We, I mean, I, just came from a sales trip to Acapulco selling woman's sportswear."

"Yes," said the officer, "but where have you *just* **come from**? "

"I gave him my most professional confused look and then repeated my story."

"That's river mud on the bottom of your car, son, so please pull your car over to that building."

He followed me on foot, ordered me out of the car and escorted me to an interrogation room. I was scared shitless. They strip-searched me and probed every orifice of my body. Then I was questioned for hours by three different officers. In the meantime, my car was being disassembled and searched. In the end they found nothing, so they could not hold me and had to let me go, but I was followed forever," Rodger rattled. "I know more about the streets of Laredo than I ever wanted to, Max. When finally, I did lose them; then headed here to try to find you, which I just amazingly did. I'll ask you this Max, though it seems all has gone well, let's not doing this again, ok?"

We waited till we were north of San Antonio before we tried out my new acquisition.

"Well Max, you're finally an independent businessman", he joked as he blew the smoke out his lips. "A real Marijuana Man. MM, creator of the Brotherhood of Smoke. Now with your straw hat and those aviator sunglasses you have a real visual mystique about you. "

"You know Rodger; what's just happen the last few days, plus what lays ahead for me, it's a lot to take in, for now and I still have a lot of logistics and planning to do, if I'm going to do this seriously and safely."

We shared silence, lost in our own thoughts, but enjoying the shared blissful enlightening high as we listen to the raspy voice of Wolf Man Jack coming from the other side of the border on Rodger's car radio.

What I had found was to be the benchmark for all marijuana in the future. So, after many years sampling many tons of products, I have found only one variety that was better than that Gold.

1967

The culture of political activism intensified with the escalation of the war in Vietnam. News coverage of social movements dominated TV screens, mingling with the blood and guts visuals of battlefields. Bloated bodies were floating in rice fields of that Asian country which seemed remote, exotic, and mostly unfamiliar to most Americans in 1967. As support for the war had dropped to just 50%, many of America's youth, especially those on college campuses, spearheaded war protest supported by prominent intellectuals, the Hollywood powerful, and sports figures.

The great Mohammad Ali refused to be inducted into the armed forces after receiving his draft notice. He was promptly arrested and convicted of draft dodging. Although his conviction was later overturned by the Supreme Court his ban from boxing coincided with arguably his best boxing year.

Martin Luther King Jr. publicly proclaimed his moral opposition to the War.

The music also represented the feeling s of the time with protesters including Joan Baez with her song "Saigon Bride," or Country Joe and the Fish's, "Feeling Like I'm Fix-in' to Die."

In late October 100,000 protesters rallied peacefully at the Lincoln Memorial, but 50,000 demonstrators proceeded to march to the Pentagon and attempted to enter the military headquarters. They were met by tear gas and arrest.

On the domestic front the National Organization for Women, NOW, pledges to fight for ratification of the Equal Rights Amendment.

The United States Supreme Court ruled to give its citizens the Maranda Act, that all suspects must be informed of their constitutional rights to an attorney, and to be protected against self-incrimination before being questioned by police.

The Civil Rights movement literally erupted into flames as race riots broke out in Ohio, and New Jersey, were but two of the over 100 riots throughout the country. These were brought on as the result of too many years of oppression, culminating in rage. The protesters and rioters destroyed their own poor neighborhoods' businesses and homes. Detroit's civil unset was quelled only after 7,000 National Guardsmen, 4700 paratroopers and 360 Michigan State Police Troopers were able to restore order. Though not before 43 individuals died, over 300 other people were wounded, and 1400 buildings were destroyed.

In California, Ronald Reagan was elected governor. In November, Senator Eugene McCarthy announced his intention to run for the U.S. Presidency with an Anti-Vietnam platform.

Once we got back to Denton, Rodger suggested we store the grass in his mom's rent house's detached garage. The old couple who were leasing the house did not have a car, so she was storing extra furnishings there. The garage opened into the alley behind the house, so I could come and go easily without drawing notice.

For his bonus in this adventure, Rodger accepted a- 2.2 pound brick.

"How long is this going to last you and all those lady buyers, Rodger? Hey, would you consider joining me in this new business? This could be our biggest adventure!"

"No thanks Max. For the time being I like hustling ladies' clothes. The side benefits have been awesome."

"Those ladies are going to be your downfall, my friend."

Over the years I would undertake equally daring enterprises, but none as stupid or ill-thought-out as that first Mexican buy. That initial trip to Mexico was just blind stupid luck. Things could have gone dreadfully wrong, but fortunately hadn't. **"Fate aids the courageous,"** As Zady would have pointed out.

Over the next several months, I would take that first $400 investment in my first Mexican deal into an $8,000 net profit. I was already getting something out of college besides a deferment and a book education; I was now officially an importer/ dealer in marijuana. Why would an enterprising entrepreneur, such as me, want to spend time in college, instead of making money full time? For most Jewish families, education is paramount. Learning and education are something you can always carry with you no matter where you go in life. Good advice and I desired to have my parents' and family's approval. Besides to augment my business, I needed a growing customer base. College students with time, some disposable income, and little supervision certainly filled that niche. But honestly, the most important and chief motivational factor for myself and many other males ages 18 to 30, was **Vietnam**. "The Draft Deferment Test," passed by the U.S. Congress in 1966, conveyed to the local draft boards that enrolled male college students would serve the nation better as a student in a classroom than as a warrior in the jungles of Vietnam. If you were a young male not enrolled in school, the odds were high that you would find yourself being drafted into the army with a gun in your hand fighting people who did not view us Americans as allies fighting communism, but rather as an invading army like the French had been, not that many years before. The Vietnam War brought more male students to college campuses than any other event since the end of World War II. Rodger and I were among them.

When I began selling ounces, I decided to set a schedule to be at a parking lot off Fry Street every Tuesday, Thursday, and Sunday morning at 10:00 to 10:40 a.m. It sounds strange, but following such a blatantly regular schedule, I did not draw attention to myself. My presence was so normal, it just seemed like I belonged there. Though I was smart enough to know when it was time to move on and to change locations, that way I could also drop problem clients, and yet keep my base happy.

One Sunday I had agreed to meet a friend to sell him a couple of lids. We met in the middle of a busy Gibson's stores parking lot. We had just finished smoking a test joint, when out of the corner of my eye. I saw a new Bright Red New Camaro recklessly driving through the lot. Only after making a couple go arounds did, he park. Out steps a 6 foot plus guy in mustard yellow, puffy -sleeved shirt, tucked in to his tight black and white bell bottom pants and held together by a thick white leather belt. The real highlight of this fashion show were the same three colors on his Beatle boots. He was shortly joined by a ragged scruffy looking soul. As they stood outside the new red car it looked like they may be doing a deal of some kind. We just stared in disbelief. As soon as money was exchanged and produced given for payment, done deal, right? No because, "The Mr. Rags" character pulls a gun and badge out and right before our eyes, Flashy is arrested. Then two black and whites pulled up and this dumbass is hauled away.

"The best lessons in life can be the ones we learn from someone else's mistakes."

From that experience I decided I needed a business plan, just like any successful business. Mine needed standard accounting, inventory control etc., but it also needed something special. My type of business need **RULES**, *guidelines*, to make the risk as small as possible, rules to keep me as safe as possible. Over the years they developed, and save my butt more than once

Rule Number One: "A nail that sticks out is just looking to be hammered."

Better be plain and fit in then bold and draw attention to yourself, and what you are doing.

Following this newly established first rule, one of the first things I did after I got back to Denton after the holidays was to sell my beloved sculptured roof '1965 Chevy 409 Impala SS to buy a 1961, nondescript, tan colored Volkswagen bus that was so generic, that it never drew attention no matter where I went.

Rule Number Two: "God speaks in still small voices…so listen."

I had not been selling lids for very long when I was asked by a ROTC type to buy four lids. From the very beginning of the introductions my hairs on my arms and neck stood straight up. And my head started pounding, and my whole being said no.!! "Sorry man I'm out, of pot and the business," turned and walked away, never looking back. Later we found out he was a snitch, for the Campus and Denton police departments. They paid him $50 per bust he helped bring in.

"Trust your gut." I have walked away from a few deals just because I got bad feelings. Your body can tell you a lot if you listen to it and the still small voice inside.

When I began selling mostly ounces, I set a schedule to be at a certain parking lot on Fry Street just off campus every Tuesday, Thursday, sand Sunday morning from 10: to 10:45 a.m. It sounds strange but following such a blatantly regular schedule. I drew no undue attention. My presence was just normal. The van also allowed me to change meeting sites if things started to get too comfy, or if I wanted to drop clients without a confrontation.

Many times, over the years I was approached and asked to sell cocaine, speed, and assorted poppy-based products. Someone even tried to force me into joining his business group. This was not for me. I saw people making lots more money off much less bulky items. As the years went by, the demand for cocaine, especially its by-products, grew larger and larger. The profit margins were greater and the prison sentences for selling it were no different than for selling pot. It was also much easier to find and already available in the U.S. All I needed was cash to buy it and clients to sell it to, I had both. Despite the economic and logistical pros of selling coca and poppy products, I turned down involvement. I was a confirmed Marijuana Man and people were still smoking marijuana. I sold pot, and there was social interaction with grass that the other drugs did not generate. There was more to my life than just money. The Brotherhood of Smoke seemed to be a social consciousness associated with us puff passers.

The New Year of 67 found me still making several forays a month to Austin to meet up with Rudy; I had no problem trading a pound of my Gold in exchange for four pounds of his street product. The Gold was so rare he was selling it for $25 per one eighth of an ounce. In the months to come I became the man to see in Denton as the underground pot-smoking clientele was growing fast. I was selling eight pounds, or one hundred twenty-eight ounces, per month. My prices rose from $15 an ounce to $18, but my buyers were not worried about price, as long as I provided the euphoric Mexican fruit. Finally, when I was buying enough quantity Rudy would make deliveries to me twice a month. I was doing well in school and making money, averaging twelve to fifteen hundred dollars a month minimum profit. My time was becoming more valuable, so I quit working at the family store on weekends, telling my folks I had found a job up in Denton, though I did not go into detail. I kept my grades up and did not ask for extra cash. No girl's father called my dad about his pregnant daughter, so all was well at my house. As the semester ended, I decided to go to the summer session. I could service the clients who had stuck around and could mellow out. I had put aside twenty pounds of grass during the year to cover my business transactions through the summer, so all was cool.

I finally decided deliveries were better made in more secure locations than my van. One of my new favorite places to conduct business during the summer term was at the university library. Often, I would bring in a lunch bag or, more recently, an old leather mail bag that I had gotten for my birthday years ago. I could conduct my business back within the stacks. No one studying in the library paid any attention to what you were doing, and the place was very quiet except when freshmen were back in the stacks, banging bones, then it could get a little bit noisy.

In the library one afternoon, I was checking out a book about flying when I noticed an attractive girl in the check-out line ahead of me. Looking over her shoulder, I noticed the title of the fat book in her hand, and asked, "Is, The *History of Baroque Chamber Music* your light reading for this evening or are you planning to use this as a doorstop for the next two weeks?" "No, I'm using it for protection against library perverts." She smiled as she turned around to reply.

"As pretty a girl as you are, maybe you need two books. My name is "Max Gold, by the way. I am a sophomore, business major." She was cute with dark brown hair and vivid blue eyes, chin-high to me and slender.

"Hello," she replied with a melodious voice. "This is for a music history class project I am working on. And my name is Debbie Cooper, freshman music major." She extended her hand. I took it in my grasp and immediately felt an electrical charge. She had a well- portioned figure; her breasts were more than a mouthful but by no means eggplants, and she had a very cute ass. As I held her hand, I noticed her simple grace and sweet laugh. "What's with the strange straw hat? And where did you get that purse Max? Really, I love it. It's just so *cool.*"

"My leather mail bag you're referring to is used to carry my important stuff. The head gear is just me." On the drive to her dorm, I found that talking to Debbie was easy.

I offered her a ride back to her dorm. On the way I found talking to Debbie was easy. "Max, my family from Fort Worth. My two older sisters, well they are trophies to their, you know doctor and lawyer husbands, like the animal heads on the walls of their homes. High-dollar breeding stock, though", she laughed. "Now my daddy rules everything and even my older brother Bud, who is in the family's money -making business with my daddy, kisses his ass. My sweet mama is just a little mouse who likes her vodka. The family has lots of money, but it has not seemed to have bought them much happiness. I'll tell you, Max, I may not know what I do want to do in my life, but I sure as hell do know what I do not want to do."

We laughed at that and then I gave her a short version of my life and family. I had to admit my family felt like a warmer and closer- knit group than hers. I did not mention my business to Debbie. We made a date for the movies that night.

Later that night after the movie *The Graduate*, I said, "We could get a bite to eat, or I could take you home or we could go back to my place and listen to some music and talk."

"Let's go back to your place so I can check out your taste in vinyl and décor," she giggled in that sweet southern girl coyness, I found so attractive.

On the way, we heard a news report about Operation Buffalo in which 159 Marines were killed, and 845 wounded. There was one MIA. Casualties on the other side, the National Vietnamese Army, were greater. 1200 were confirmed dead but another 513 could likely be added to the list. The U.S. succeeded in destroying 164 enemy bunkers and 15 artillery and rocket positions. At least 100 weapons were confiscated. This prompted a discussion about the Vietnam War and the 500,000 troops in that country. Debbie supported the peace movement that was spreading across the county. Rallies, like the one in San Francisco at Keizer Stadium where 40,000 people gathered to voice their opinion, stirred the strong feelings that she freely expressed to me. "Max, we have no business sending our strongest and brightest youth to fight a war that is only meant to put profits into the military complex. That's what president Eisenhower warned us about. Their profits are being fed by our young men's blood." She was getting no augment from me.

When we got to my small house west of campus, Debbie found my décor to consist of mostly old hand me-downs and a few old wooden pieces picked up from a local used furniture store. After we completed the two-second tour, and when we reached the stereo I choose the Beatle's, "Sgt. Pepper's Lonely Heart Band", from my collection of albums, then suavely sat down next to Debbie on the old worn sofa covered with an Indian, printed cloth, to cover a couple stains and a burn mark.

"Talking about dangerous situations, I joked, I noticed you smoke. Haven't you read the hazardous warning labels Congress now has on these new packs?"

She covered her ears with her hands. "Yeah, yeah, I'm going to quit, lalalala."

"Well, if you must smoke, at least try my private brand." I pulled out from my leather mailbag a twisted bird of Gold, lit it, smiled and said, "Alright, Debbie, hold on to your seat." I showed her how to hold the joint and showed her how to inhale and hold in the smoke. Like most novices, she drew too hard, drawing more smoke than her lungs could handle. She coughed, and coughed, and coughed. "Good stuff?" I innocently asked.

She simply nodded, wiped away a tear that was slowly leaking out of her eyelid, and then took a couple more hits before a sip of water. She leaned her head against my shoulder and closed her eyes. I noticed her fingers unconsciously began to move in time to the music, instantly day tripping. When "Sergeant Pepper" ended, she sighed, "That was amazing."

"So, tell me, what happened? Where did you go? What did you think about it? What did you hear?" I asked.

"I'll tell you in a minute Max, but um… do you have anything to eat? I'm famished and still have dry mouth." Sitting at the bar which separated the small kitchen from the living area, we laughed till we hurt while we pigged out on potato chips, onion dip, and chocolate chip cookies.

"I saw the orchestra as if I was the conductor. I felt the wand in my hand. I heard it swishing through the air. I wanted nothing more than to be right where I 'm at now, relaxed, yet energized at the same time."

"Mellow," I interjected.

"Now I really understand that word. If we could get everyone to smoke this herb, world peace would be inevitable."

I agreed, "If you wrapped your hand around a pipe or lit a joint, and filled your lungs with smoke, a gun and its violence would hold no charm, I would think."

We listened to her favorite female singer, Mama Cass of the Mamas and Papas, followed by the Rolling Stones' new album, *Between the Buttons*. My turn again. I chose the great musical poet, Bob Dylan's classic, "*The Times They are a-Changin,*" *and as* a hot-rod guy, the Beach Boys, "Smile."

Debbie said, "Do you know what I like about you Max?" I just shook my head. "Well, besides being cute and having a funky bus, you do not brag about yourself or start every sentence with the word, 'I.' You ask my opinion, and most importantly, you actually listen to what I have to say when I'm talking. You have not groped, grabbed, pressed me, or made me feel uncomfortable."

"Ah…well… My mom has raised me to be a gentleman with women of all ages and to treat you all as I would treat her.

Debbie next requested Simon and Garfunkel's *The Sound of Silence*. "I can't wait until *The Graduate* sound track comes out. She lit a cigarette, lifted her leg and placed her foot on my lap and began to massage my sleeping manhood.

"Mrs. Robinson, are you trying to seduce me?"

Any sex is enjoyable, but sex on Acapulco Gold is spectacular.

The next morning as I got out of bed with a neck full of Hickie's, Debbie said, "Max, last night was wonderful. Introducing me to pot is the best thing anyone has ever done for me. Weed is so much better than liquor or cigarettes. I want more, lots more. Where did you get it? How can I get some?"

I just smiled. "I'll take care of you in that department, Kido." I figured I might as well tell her what I was really up to; she would figure it out soon enough on her own. So, I sat down on the edge of the bed. "I need to talk to you, Debs. I already have strong feelings for you and think you need should know how I pay my bills." if we are going to continue our relationship, you need to know the truth, so you can decide if you want to continue with me or not." I took a deep breath and began, "I am a marijuana dealer."

I watched her face. She froze. I saw her pupils widen and she stopped blinking for a moment. "Oh," was all she said.

"I will never involve you in any of this business, and I'll never put you at risk. Debbie, if this is going to cause you a problem I understand. If you want to think this through or if you want to back out, I will accept your decision and not bother you ever again." All of this rushed out of me in one long breath. "But I think you need the truth. I'll answer any questions I can for you now but after today I will not talk about it, it's for your own safety."

She asked me a jillion question; she was very bright and quick. I answered them as best as I could, but when I did not answer a question, she seemed to understand why. "Where do you get it? How much money are you making off each? Do you sell it like cigarettes in packs of just one at a time? Aren't you afraid of getting caught?" One question led to at least two more.

Finally, I said, "I have a set of rules which I use to live by for my own protection. For example, I do not conduct business here at home nor do I store my inventory here. I also do not take phone calls for or about business here at the house." I have a set schedule. If you want pot that's the only time, I'm available. I don't want people showing up all day and night looking for a score. If you want my grass, it is my way or no way.

I only keep enough marijuana here at the house for my personal use. That's here or in the van when I am not delivering.

Rule Number Three: "Cast no stone into a well that gives you water."

Do not conduct business or keep inventory at your residency.

Debbie sat quietly for a few moments looking deeply into my eyes, saying nothing. Finally, after what seemed like a lifetime. "Max, you should have said something before I started liking you." She paused and looked down. My heart pounded. Slowly she raised her head, grinned, and surprised me by leaning forward to kiss me. "I'm honored that you have such trust in me. It means a lot."

Debbie took my hand, "Max, since you have been so open; let me share some of my family's history with you. In the '20s during Probation, my mom's dad Samuel smuggled illegal liquor from Mexico. That is where the family got its seed money. Gramps took his large profits and invested in the early stages of the East Texas oil and gas industry and then land. My daddy was just an oil field ruff neck when he met my mother. Then my dad had gramps' money to buy us respectability." So, it seemed I was just continuing her family's legacy.

We had lots of together time when not in our classes, and it was shortly after our first month together, when I began seeing small changes in her, at first it did not concern me she was growing as a person with and without the weed in her. One of the first things she joined and then would become a leader of, was a women's campus organization to support and fight for the passage of the ERA, the Equal Rights Amendment. The legislation would guarantee no one could be discriminated against based on gender. Then Debbie changed from a dress and pumps, always in make-up kind of girl, to one that used no make-up, and now wore tie-dyed gauze tops to cover her newly freed braless breast. A few weekends earlier she and the members of her ERA group held a protest in front of the administration building and had a mass bra burning ceremony. I am a red-blooded guy and a big, big fan of untethered breasts, but it seemed my Debbie had gone from prom queen to Grace Slick overnight. The marijuana had opened a door for her, and her former self seemed to have disappeared in the smoke, but the women that did emerge was a stronger and more powerful women, whose convictions were forming even as we spoke, and they were getting stronger by the week.

But when she was not in classes or meetings, or out of town demon-stration, we found ourselves hanging out together as young lovers do, Sex, Marijuana and Rock-an-Roll was our theme. She visited the school clinic for birth control pills. We certainly did not want the unexpected arrival of any little Maxes or Debbie's to cramp our style. We spent most of our free time together unless her folks insisted that she come home for a weekend. Other than those occasions, she would check out of her dorm Friday and return Sunday evenings.

After summer school ended but before the Fall Semester, 1967-68 began, I had a few weeks free. One morning Rodger came by the house excited. "Max, I think I have a great lead to a new supplier for you in Dallas. I've been dating a girl off and on. Her little brother and I smoke sometimes. He said his supplier let it slip that he has just scored from a new dealer in Dallas. His name is Dirk, and he has a small beer joint in Dallas.

The dealer Rodger had referenced owned a working guy's bar on Harry Hines Boulevard. As I pulled off my aviators, I could see it was strictly blue collar, redneck place with peanuts for appetizers. The discarded shells covering the floor, were its décor. The place had a couple of pool tables in the back corner, and it had many well-worn bar stools and a few equally worn booths. The Wurlitzer played Willy, Waylon and Jerry Jeff, along with Merle and, of course, Hank Williams. The drink for that day, and any day, was the King of Beers, Budweiser. Even in my straw hat, I felt like I stuck out. I went to the bar and got a draw, then sat down in a booth to watch two guys pound the balls around the stained and faded green felt. This was the bar's ambiance, along with the smell of stale beer and sweaty bodies. The only other person, besides the pool players and me, was the bartender who came over to ask if I needed a refill. "I'll take another and is Dirk around?" I asked.

"Who should I say is calling?" he asked.

My mind went blank, and then out of my mouth came, "Tell him MM from Denton would like a moment of his time." I was flying by the seat of my pants, but it sure sounded better than Max Gold from North Dallas. The funny thing is I had never used that name before and had only heard it used once by Rodger all those months ago. The name, "MM" was to become my shortened handle. Even today I'll run into someone who will still call me that.

He looked me in the eye, winked and then went up the stairs against the dark wall. He was gone but a few seconds when he came back down and told me, "Go ahead up."

As I climbed the squeaky stairs, my adrenaline kicked in; my heart was beating out of my chest it seemed, and I hoped the guy on the other side of this door would not notice. I knocked on the door and from the other side a voice beckoned me, "Coomme oon in". As I opened the door, I had no idea what awaited me or what to expect. I stepped into a nearly bare office. There were two folding chairs, an old oak desk with a few pictures on it, a couple of baseball plaques and an old faded brown sofa behind a glass coffee table beneath a small window._I recognized Dirk as a guy who I did not know personally but had seen on campus at some school sporting events. I think he had been a big jock on campus, so we really did not have a lot in common, until now. He held out his hand. "Dirk," he said as we shook.

"Max," I countered.

"M M, the Marijuana Man of Denton Texas? I actually have heard of you, Max, and I have to tell you, I admire your style. You seem to have your business under control, no heat. Some of our mutual customers speak very highly of you." I thanked him and sat back to think about that for a while. "I had actually planned to run you down, or at least put the word out after school started. Max, I don't want to do any more retail business; I have a great source now and just want to move pounds from now on. I'll leave you all the crazies and yahoos, thank you very much. Besides I don't want to end up like young Tom King", he laughed. "You heard the story, right?"

I had been told one by Rudy, a rumored story of some outsider from the North selling wet hybrid weed that was like bad news and he got caught. "Yeah, but what did you hear?"

"Well, the story I was told was from someone who claims they were there. A rich kid from upper state New York was driving to Austin to return to the University of Texas for fall classes. While driving through Ohio, outside of Columbus he noticed marijuana growing wild on the side of the road. It went for miles. He pulled over to inspect and, what he found was a short, stubby marijuana plant in full bloom, the buds covered with resin. He turned around and headed to the nearest town. He rented an enclosed trailer and bought garden tools. He spent the better part of the night cutting and loading buds and plants. When he reached Austin none of the fall Mexican harvest had made to town yet. His wet weed sold quickly. The story goes he cleared over $50,000 in just a few weeks. The problem though, this weed was Ditch Weed. A cross of Marijuana and the native Hemp plant, it has very little THC or buzz juice, and it smokes like rope. My guy claimed he and a group of his Frat brothers escorted him out of town only after they tarred and feathered him."

"The story I heard, they cut is Dick off, but in any case. If I run into any disgruntled clients of that nature, I'll give them your name and number before they do it to me." We both just smiled. When it comes to customers, well that's why I am so picky about whom I sell it to. There are plenty of people who want what we sell. I'm not looking just to sell as much as I can, just as much as I safely can. I'll miss one if I don't feel right about it. That way I can sleep easily at night."

I could see his point though I liked the comradery I had with my customers. I am not just their dealer friend. Many had become my friends as well I was a friend who was a spreader of knowledge or so it seemed at the time.

Rule Number Four: Know as much as you can about each of your customers.

It is very important in any business to have as many customers or clients as possible, but "not all customers are equal, and some are best to avoid doing any business with at all." **"If you give a pig a chair, next he will want to dance on the table."** They are dangerous and are a threat to themselves as well as those around them. I only sold to people I directly knew or who were referred to by an existing customer. There was such a demand on the retail level that I could be picky about who I sold to, and I never ran out of demand before I ran out of the product.

"Right, I feel I have less risk selling twenty-five-pound minimums than I do selling lids." Then I could see his point too.

I pulled out a joint of my Gold and with his okay, sparked it up. This smoke sealed our deal. We discussed price, quantity, and when and where to pick up. He was going down South to make a pickup the next week, so we made a tentative pick-up date and time. I was to call at the end of the next week to confirm we were still on. Though I was buying a lot more of the product at one time than before, my cost through Dirk would be cheaper than I had been paying Rudy and the trip to Dallas was much closer than to Austin if I had to make a run.

"Max, I have just two questions for you. Where did you get the stuff, we just smoked and where can I get some?" Dirk asked.

I just smiled and said, "That's a story for another time but I've got you covered on the other."

My fifty- pound load of marijuana was to be picked up at an old warehouse just south of downtown Dallas. The purchase price was $75 per pound, cash. I also threw in a lid of my Gold to sweeten the deal for Dirk as promised. I had found a great marketing idea, borrowing from the donut business: a baker's dozen, or thirteen for the price of twelve. Something for nothing always makes the recipient feel like he has gotten a better deal than expected and makes for a loyal customer, or in this case, a loyal supplier.

At the designated time, I showed up. The warehouse where we had arranged to meet had large doors, so I could just pull in with my van. Dirk and his bartender, who turned out to be his brother- in-law, were both wearing holstered .38s on their hips, and I also noticed a shotgun leaning against the wall. In the middle of the warehouse was an old wooden desk on which was a beam scale, and next to the desk my fifty pounds of marijuana, wrapped in brick packages, were neatly stacked on the floor. Each of the butcher-papered bricks had its weight written on the outside. I opened a few bricks to make sure of what I was buying and that they were not filled with sticks and stems. I also weighed six or seven different blocks to make sure the weights matched what was written on the bundle. A short discussion followed regarding the weight of paper I was paying for. "I pay for it, so you pay for it. It's just another, cost of doing business Max," other than that all else checked out. I loaded up with their help, and after my cash was counted, I was gone. I was in and out in less than fifteen minutes; this was not the time to stick around and socialize.

I had to keep the windows up due to the smell while I cruised back to Denton just below the speed limit, not wanting to get stopped by John Law. I do not know if it was the heat inside my bus or the vapor coming off the bricks, but I was almost hallucinating by the time I got back to Denton.

After that, Ole MM would carry his own scales. Though, after years of doing so, I could tell by handling them if the bricks were okay or if there was some foreign matter inside the packaging. As the cost of marijuana went up over the years, I had to be careful that I was not paying high dollars for paper packaging and lots of woody stems. This happened only occasionally with my suppliers, but when it did, I would have to adjust my price to my customer or replace an entire brick if they found too much trash inside. Not acceptable.

On occasion I had bought what looked like good grass, but in reality, it was of poor quality, probably harvested too early, before the plant was ready. I had to adjust my prices or make a bunch of hash or brownies out of the trash weed. Sometimes you can't tell the quality of the product until you smoke it, but you cannot smoke even a little of every brick you buy. I have smoked pot that looked great, big buds, lots of rusty-looking hairs, even tasted ok, but I had to smoke a lot to get even a little buzz, and then ended up with a headache. Other times some very nasty-looking wild weed that looked like dried, cooked spinach and tasted like what I imagine eating dog shit might be like, but after a hit or two, I was in La-La land. You just don't know until you heat it up.

I remember Zady's business and personal philosophy. "Max listen to me," he'd say, "It takes minutes, hours, days, weeks, months, years to make a good customer or great friend, but only seconds to lose them."

Rule Number Five: Sell what you know or know what you sell.

Most of the smoke I bought had lots of seeds in the buds. This meant that the plant was a female and was grown outside with male plants around to fertilize the females. The premium marijuana in is "Sinsemilla," which does not have developed seeds in the buds. This indicates that the female plants have not been exposed to the male's pollen, causing the female plant to continue to produce more and more THC potent resin in an effort to collect additional pollen from the environment even when there is none. It's like the perfume women wear to attract the male species. In essence, the plant flourishes even though there are no male plants. This makes a great product and the most sought- after type of grass that goes for more money per ounce with no superfluous seed weight. Since most Mexican farmers are interested in producing weight and bulk with the least amount of effort, they do not take the time or expense to cut male plants down.

When I arrived back to my small two- bedroom house from the warehouse with the fresh buy, I was greeted by Rodger and Debbie who had already the dining room table covered with newspaper, the scale and baggies waiting to be filled. They were both excited to view my new purchase and to try out the new weed, fresh from the fields.

"What's going on?" I asked surprised to see Rodger and Debbie," What are you two doing here? You can't be here Debs, it's not safe you should go home, and I'll pick you up later.

"No Max, if Rodger is in, then so am I. I have tons of girlfriends who will buy all day long besides if I don't get it from you, I'll get it elsewhere and you know I will."

"What about you Rodger, are you in too?"

"Yeah, the driving, living on the road, wakening up next to who I don't remember, is getting old, so let's make this happen, what's yah got MM?"

I had brought in a couple of bricks. "Okay, kids, you get to christen this year's fresh crop, Catch." It was funny to watch them rip apart the bricks like a kids opening birthday gifts. It did not take Rodger much time before he had a fat one rolled, lit, and passed. "The boy has promise," I announced as I went for a big bowl.

"What's the bowl for?" asked Rodger, as he puffed away.

"Well, I'll tell you I'm going to start collecting the loose seeds that we have been throwing away all this time. They may have no value, but I have an idea in the back of my mind, so I've been collecting them for a while. "But Debbie, I wish you would reconsider this, the possible consequences, and all."

"Thanks Max but I have put a lot of thought to this; the money I make will help my cause." I did not ask which one it was, this week.

We spent the next few hours bagging up one-ounce bags. I pulled out several fresh long, full buds to use as samples to show friends and a few picky clients. We rolled a couple more joints to enjoy while we worked.

Rule Number Six: "He who wishes to be wise should study monetary laws."

"All right, Rodger, here is the system I want us to use in checking out each brick in storage. Write down the weight that is written on each of these bundles. In this spiral notebook we will make a list of the individual weights of the packages. In the next column we will put the dates on which a bundle is removed. Second, I do not want more than one or two bricks, at the most, to be taken out at a time. This might be an illegal business, but it is still a business, and we need to keep an eye on the accounting; otherwise, you do not know where you are or where you are going. Last, I want your account paid up by the end of each week, Okay?" Rodger looked up and just nodded. I never had any problem with Rodger's honesty. If he took out product, he followed the procedures and paid his bills no later than every Sunday night as he had agreed to. "And you, young lady, we'll sit down, you and I, to work some sort of arrangement like Rodgers to fit your needs.

"Thank you, Maxie", she then gave me her coyly smile and went back to her packing and weighing.

We drove a couple of miles to unload the remainder of the marijuana in Rodger's mother's unused rent house garage. We stacked the bricks on a tabletop and covered the grass with a canvas painter's drop cloth to help keep the smell down. I also added several new boxes of rat poison around the interior to feed the vermin that might be drawn to the new marijuana.

The Boy Scouts had taught me to **"Be prepared,"** so that same week, I also spent some money to meet with a very good criminal attorney, Abe "the Barbarian" Blend, in Dallas, to get some basic information about what to expect if one of us got arrested and what action we should take to protect ourselves in that worst- case scenario. It was two hundred dollars well spent and, though I did not have him on retainer, I knew that if I called him in the future, Abe would already have a good idea why.

When I returned from my meeting with the Barbarian, I sat down with Rodger and Debbie, and I went over what I'd learned from my new adviser, so in the end we all could be informed if the worst happened. "First, do not fight the arrest. Second, say nothing more than your name and request a call to your attorney. *Then keep your mouth shut, and keep your mouth shut. Lastly, keep your mouth shut.*" Rodger would follow my directives and set up some sort of system that worked well for him, and he, in turn, sold a lot of grass and had no problems with the police or DEA.

Debbie did bring a scare to us both once. The mother of a girl who she had sold a lid to called her and chewed Debbie out to sell her daughter the grass. She went over to her house right away and gave the mother twenty dollars cash back and apologized, she was wearing one of her ERA "Tee's", so things went smoothly. But we still held our breaths for several weeks, waiting for a police car to meet her at the dorm. Fortunately, nothing further resulted from this incident, but you never can tell what is going to spark the interest of the police. As much as possible I wanted to keep the business away from my personal life.

One late August afternoon, Rodger was over at my small house in Denton when the air conditioning went out. We had to open the windows and use fans to try to keep cool. In Texas the summer temperature averages in the upper 90s. We had been listening to some new tunes when the needle broke on the record player's tone arm. Rodger made a loud obscene comment which could be heard over Bob Dylan with regard to where he would like to stick this needle. I changed the needle to a new one and we settled in to listen to Dylan's "Like a Rolling Stone". About an hour later two of Denton's finest in blue appeared at my door. "Mr. Gold, we received a call from one of your neighbors that drugs use is going on in this home." I had just "cleaned house" and had thrown away all my pot trash so thankfully, the house was clean. The other officer mentioned that the neighbors reported hearing a remark about a "broken needle."

Rodger's face showed instant relief and put the wind back in my sail." Officer," I explained, "The stereo broke its needle and my buddy here Roger has been yelling at the turntable." At that one of the officers smiled and shook his head. After a quick look around, they thanked us and left.

Rule Number Seven: "Draw from the past, live in the present, work for the future."

I had to keep in control after the first Denton incident I never left as much as a roach clip, rolling papers or unfinished joint out. There was another time, a couple years later, when Rodger and I were living in an apartment together in Dallas. It was at the end of August and Rodger's girlfriend at the time, Wendy, was staying with us until school started and she could move into campus housing. She was from Pittsburgh and had all of her pots and pans, kitchenware and furniture stored in our living room and in Rodger's bedroom. Our place looked like a flea market that was hit by a tornado. Our second-floor apartment had a balcony that overlooked the swimming pool and also served the next-door apartment. One Sunday morning I answered a knock on the front door only to find two of Dallas's finest in blue, police officers. There had been a break- in at the next-door apartment and since our balconies adjoined, they would like to check out our back door to see if it had been the access point into the apartment next door. We had a little weed in one of the kitchen drawers, but I knew that if I said no, that they would come back with a warrant and really tear the place apart and would surely find at least one seed or a roach somewhere if they looked hard enough.

41 |

"Come in officers and look at whatever you need to." I smiled and invited them in. One of the officers went next door and brought the two neighbor girls in to check Wendy's stuff out for their missing goods. The officers searched a few drawers but not the one with my stash and after the girls did not find any of the missing items, they left along with the two officers after the senior policeman thanked me for the cooperation. My paranoia and strict adherence to the rules paid off again.

Just before the fall semester ended in 1967, I got approached by Billy Williams, a classmate of mine from a freshman accounting class.

"Hey Max, do you have time for a cup of coffee? I have a proposition for you." We went to a small diner just off campus. "My father died a couple of months ago Max and the bank, which we use to borrow money for seed, fertilizer and working capital to hold us through until harvest time, now wants the money back that they had lent dad for this year's broom corn crop." This type of sorghum is used for making brooms and grows from six to fifteen feet tall. "Most of the cash from the broom crop has already been spent on the seed and fertilizer, so the bank wanted to foreclose on the loan and take my family's farm," Billy recounted.

"Sad story," I said. "But what can I do for you?"

He smiled and went back to his story. "I got the bank to hold off until next fall's harvest, but I know it's a long shot that we will even make enough to cover the interest on the loan, let alone the original amount. It would take a miracle for the price of broom corn and sorghum to rise high enough to make the profit we would need. So, I was thinking, if you could get me cannabis seeds? I can plant them in the middle of the broom corn where the plants will be hidden. After summer harvest, I will sell you the pot harvest." I was taken back at first that he already seemed to have it all worked out. I asked a lot of questions for which he had the right answers. "Cannabis is a member of the hemp family which my grandfather grew on the property many years ago. Our farm is located way out in a rural county in the panhandle of Oklahoma. We have very little traffic or airplanes flying overhead. Look, Max, you hardly know me, but I am in a bind. I am not a drug-type guy, but I have my mom, a little brother and two sisters. This farm has been in the family since the late 1880s, Sooners--Boomer's days, and this is all we have. I need the seeds and a place to sell the crop for cash when it is harvested. Can you help me out?

"How much do you think you could grow and harvest?" I asked.

"At least two to four thousand pounds; I don't know, maybe more, depending on how many seeds you can get. I'm used to dealing in bushels, not pounds, and I still have to work out how to harvest it. I don't think you would want it in fifty-pound bales, would you?"

I just shrugged my shoulders. I had never considered that marijuana might come in any other type of packaging than one pound to 2.2 # Kilo bricks. Bigger bundles might work. "I'll get back to you on that," I laughed. I've got some seeds, and if I check around maybe I can dig you up some more," I answered excitedly. We worked out a price of $30 a pound for tops, no male plants, no large stems, and no Oklahoma red dirt. "Billy, the last thing to discuss is the facts that if you should, in a worse- case scenario, you get busted. Well, that's all about you until I take possession. After that, it's on me and you do not have to worry, okay?" I did have one worry. What if I got him the seeds, but he sold the harvest to someone else for more money? I had met a lot of people during the last year and a half and had learned to be a pretty good judge of people. Billy was a country boy who grew up working his ass off from a young age, like me at our family store. I trusted him, and this could benefit both of us.

We shook hands and had our agreement, and I told him, "I'll stay in touch." But then I had to work digging up seeds, lots and lots of seeds, from every connection I had. It seems people often save their seeds for future fantasy farms. The one thing I never asked Billy is how did he know to come to me for this deal?

Everyone I approached had seeds. Getting them to let go of them was another story. I had to promise a lot of super-duper deals on the harvested product in return for their seed stash. With a few the only way was a pound–for- pound exchange of seed pounds for ripe bud pounds, a simple exchange. It took me a while, but I managed to come up with about fifty pounds of mostly Mexican, but it probably contained a mix of various types.

Billy was talking about a one hundred twenty-thousand-dollar cash, payday, maybe more, which was way out of my budget, but I felt that Juan or Dusty might be interested in the deal or at least a piece of it.

I had promised to sell over a thousand pounds just to the people I had gathered seeds from. At ninety dollars a pound, delivered, I would still make a very good return on time. The opportunity for such a quick profit opened my eyes to a better way to be a Marijuana Man. I remembered what Dirk, my Dallas bar-owning supplier, had said to me when we first met: **"Less risk, more profit."** My business plan was about to evolve. I learned a lot in my NSTU business classes about manufacturing, supply and demand, marketing, advertising, and most importantly, accounting. My own business gave me a reason to practice these lessons in real life.

1967 to 1968 selling season went very well, for Rodger, Debbie and I, at least we had no major problems on that front. I still bought some weed from my Austin supplier for fill-in when Dirk was out. Rudy was always a treat, and we became close friends. He would call me when he was heading our way to Dallas or up to Oklahoma. I was often his last stop, and he would spend the night sometimes. Rudy was a very funny guy and always had a joke or two to keep us laughing. One night he told one of his best. "Well guys you see I have a cousin, Charity. She's a 38-year-old single woman who happens to be very large. When she lost her job, she had to move back in with her parents, my aunt and uncle. Charity had been home for about a week when my aunt was walking down the hall past her room with its closed door. She heard a strange buzzing and moaning coming from the other side of the door, so her curiosity got the better of her. She pushed the door open and stuck her head in. What she saw completely embarrassed her. Charity was busy working a vibrator on her sex. My aunt screamed, "What are you doing?"

My cousin looked up. "Look mom, I am thirty-eight years old. I am never going to be a size 10 ever again, and I'm never getting married, so this is my husband. Just leave me alone." Later that same week my uncle was walking past Charity's closed door when he heard deep moaning and a vibrating sound. He opened the door without knocking and found his daughter using the vibrator on herself.

"What, why, aaah, ", he mumbled, in a rush of words as he quickly turned his head.

'Look pop I am nearly forty years old, I got no life, and I'm not getting married, so this is my husband so please leave me the hell alone."

The following Sunday my aunt was passing the den when she heard the TV and the now familiar buzzing. She walked into the den to find my uncle there with a beer in one hand and the now famous, penis-shaped vibrator in the other. My aunt stepped in front of my uncle and asked. "Just what in the world are you doing?"

"Look, woman," he easily replied, "can't you tell I'm watching the game with my son-in-law!"

Rudy, Debbi and Rodger and I laughed so hard we had a hard time breathing and I nearly peed myself.

Rudy always had something to put a smile on our faces. But besides that, story, he also hooked me up with a great contact for high-grade, exotic marijuana. The contact was named Dusty Dan who lived in Houston. He handled only very high-end sinsemilla strains of marijuana and hash, THC oils, mescaline buds, psychedelic mushrooms and LSD. His products came from Jamaica, Afghanistan, Thailand, India, Africa and anywhere else that was out of the ordinary. His product started at one hundred and sixty dollars an ounce and went up from there.

When we were out to dinner that night, Rudy used the pay phone to set up my first visit to Dan. I was able to swap some of the last of my Gold for a few samples of his variety for my personal stash. Whenever I had high-end buyers for whom money was not a problem, Dan was my man. He told me that every year he would travel to different parts of the world and spend time looking for unusual reefer and expand his contact network. He was able to work something out with airline personnel to bring it into Houston. The amounts were not large poundage, so they were never searched. He told me that on a few occasions he would actually mail it back to himself with other items he had purchased on the trip. Dan was to allow me to expand my business to a high-end clientele.

Dallas has several men's and women's clothing trade shows a year to which buyers and sellers come from all over the United States. The sellers from both coasts came in with plenty of cash to spend on entertainment. Rodger got me into a few shows and introduced me around. From that point on it was like shooting fish in a barrel. The cash flew into my pockets; everybody loved Dusty Dan's product lines. After the first show I got referrals from my men's line guy to their friends who sold women's wear and they were even bigger consumers during market weeks, so I always stocked up for markets, and over the years, I made a lot of money off them.

1968

January 31, 1968 Viet Nam's most celebrated national holiday the New Year **Tet** *started. It also was the beginning of the Viet Cong's Tet Offence, stating with an 18 man suicide attack on the American embassy, though it was a failure. The American people back home saw for the first time how we were very venerable, and the war maybe not going as we had been told. It was just one attack of many that the North's used in many of the souths major cities. So as to show us, 'we can not only defend our country, but push back and we will bring the fight to you to in the South.' They hoped to rally their southern brothers to join them in revolt.*

*Rev. **Martin Luther King Jr.,** the courageous Civil Rights leader, was assassinated in Memphis, Tennessee, outside his motel room. The sniper, James Earl Ray, would latter confess to the murder when he was caught in London two months later. His sentence was for ninety-nine years.*

The reaction of most American people to the death of Martin Luther King Jr was like when we found out about the assassination of President John Kennedy, disbelieve. Though his death, did give fuel to the angry minority and fires burning in many cities, then race riots broke out. Even in our own capital, Washington D.C. For the next five days, Chicago, Baltimore, Los Angles, and Memphis were among with a few of the troubled cities that had racial disturbances.

Smartly, using the memory of Dr. King, for what he had done for mankind and to show unity for the cause of freedom for all men of all color throughout the whole world. President Johnson took the opportunity and timing as only he could, to push through his "Civil Rights Act of 1968" in record time. It was a completed dream for both men. The country shut down for a few days and there were many protest marches throughout America. This tragedy gave great momentum to protesters who were making great strides, for the Civil Rights Movement and brought long-awaited changes for many people.

Presidential candidate, Senator Robert Kennedy's was shot and serious wounding in an assassination attempt, dying of those gunshot wounds the next day.

Dr. Martin Luther King's assassination drew us back to our TV's, playing non-stop, as the public was starving for any tidbits of information. "Max, I don't understand this world why are the really good people being murdered? Debbie's perspective of life though was being reshaped every day little by little. Debbie respected Dr. King and his nonviolent message.

The student and faculty march for the memory of Dr. King and in honor of what he had done for mankind and to show unity for the cause of freedom for all men, of all color throughout the whole world without using violence. It turned out to be huge. Students and faculty of Texas Woman's University also joined the event and people from all around Denton joined in a communal experience. An experience like that does not come often in one's life. As we marched, some people carried peace signs, and others had civil right quotes like "We shall overcome "and "Stop the War" At the end after all the speeches by the "Who-ever," the crowd continued to march peacefully around the campus. That day is one I'll never forget; the only regret I have is I wish I could have handed out joints and added a light-up to this event, which would really have brought peace and harmony, at least to this small part of the world.

Rule Number: Eight "When the opportunity arrives at your door, offer him a chair."

The rest of the 1968 semester I found my retail client base still growing weekly, and I even sold a few pound orders to folks who were heading back home for the semester break. Rodger even brought in a guy who ordered 100 pounds to take back to Brooklyn. One of my new friends caught me in a weaker moment, paid me half of what he owed for his purchase before he left for home and was to bring back the balance when he came back. He never came back. I tried to run him down, but it turned out he was not even a student at NTSU, and no one really knew who he was or where he was from. Why does it always cost so much to learn another life lesson? In the long run it was a cheap lesson of a couple of lost pounds.

During the late spring of 1968, I made a few weekend trips to area college campuses to try to make future contacts for my new fall business plans. My last stop was at Tyler Junior College in East Texas. Rodger had met a clothing buyer's mother who ran an apartment complex. She was also a bootlegger, supplier of hard liquor, beer and wine to customers because Tyler was in a dry county. Selling pot, sure no problem. I also made a great connection in Norman, and in Stillwater Oklahoma, run by twin brothers who were running a very stealth set of operations. We were to become good lifetime friends. Also, I made a super connection through an old high school friend in Fayetteville, Arkansas. It was not hard to hook up with dealers, on almost any campus, the marijuana-smoking population was a growing one, and a few properly asked questions usually got me a name or two which would lead to a new buyer who was always looking for a better supplier who could sell at a lower price. Some of these contacts I would work with for many years. Others I would get bad feelings about or just consider too flaky to ever call back. I never gave anyone my phone number or another way to reach me; I would always get back to them. I also used rental cars on these fishing expeditions.

When the Oklahoma broom corn and cannabis did come in, I would have at least several good names of cash buyers.

At the end of the spring semester 68, Debbie moved in with me. She met my family earlier when my sister and her family had come to Dallas for a visit, and my brother Danny had come from Austin on a rare visit. My parents and siblings made it a point to be friendly toward Debbie, not just because she was my girlfriend, but because that is just the way they were with their guests. My sister really engaged Debbie by talking about piano lessons for my oldest niece. The tween was more interested in talking about Elvis Presley's upcoming wedding. My dad and Debbie discussed the book they both had read, Ralph Nader's "*Unsafe at Any Speed,*" an indictment of the American automobile manufacturers' lack of concern with safety issues. But my mom and Debbie had the most in common. They shared a love for classical music, and anything related to the arts. My mom had just heard some cuts from the Beatles' newest album, 'SGT. Pepper's Lonely Heart Club Band', and really liked how they combined different types of music and instruments in this album. That and the fact my mom was also involved with the ERA. Well two peas in the same classy pod.

On the other hand, our cohabitation majorly upset her parents. I knew that they hated me just because I was not a WASP and had the last name Gold. I had only met them once when Debbie and I had gone to a birthday celebration for her mom at their country club. I dressed up in white button-down shirt, dark blue sports coat and white slacks, had gotten my hair trimmed and had a clean-shaven face. I was not the California hippie that had seduced their little girl as they had envisioned. Debbie was touched by the effort I had put into getting cleaned up. I really wanted to impress her family and make things go smoothly for Debbie's sake. Her dad took one look at me and mumbled, "Hello."

I extended my hand and introduced myself, "Max Gold, sir," I had never felt such a fishy handshake in my life. I always feel you can tell a lot about a person by how they shake your hand. I don't know how the guy could have been successful in business with that handshake if he used it on everyone he met.

Debbie's mom gave me a small, smirked smile and a polite, "Hello." No, "glad to meet you. We have heard so much about you. Debbie is so happy", etc. Her brother, sisters and their spouses just kind of ignored me. In fact, I had more conversations with the bartender than with any of the family though I just ordered one drink. Debbie was very embarrassed by her family's behavior and apologized several times that night on the way home.

When Debbie's folks found out that her new address, a small frame house, was going to be the same as mine, her dad went ballistic. Over the phone he went so far as to threaten Debbie with cutting off her financial support. She sat in front of me and bawled as she told me of the conversation with her dad. "Look, Debbie," I said, "First, you have a scholarship for school tuition. Second, your grandfather left you a trust fund which is yours, not anyone else's. You can keep some of your dealing cash instead of giving it all away. And, finally, you are living here, so I'll cover all the rest." She thought about it for a while. Stiffening her back, gave me a hug and then went to call her dad back and really chewed him out. "I am a grown woman and do not need your permission about what to do with my life. If you think you can control me through money, it is not going to work. I'll tell you what you can do with your money." He was on the losing end of that fight and in the end did not want to alienate his daughter for good. Her dad continued to send her money, but it was to cost him in regard to their relationship. I believe that this face-off between Debbie and her folks was one that would have happened even if there had never been Max Gold in her life; she was becoming a very strong- willed, self-sufficient lady.

Wednesday June 5 was a rainy day and Deb's, and I had nothing big planned, so we were inside, where we were feeding our flesh and smoking up our minds. Our top conflict was which radio station to listen to, when the current one that was on, announced: **"Robert Kennedy has been shot in a California Hotel while campaigning for President of the United States."** We quickly turned on the TV and again time stood still; it would not be until the next day that Robert would die from his gun shots wounds. Once again, the nation is stuck in the room where the TV is played non-stop, the public starving for any tidbits of information. "Max, I don't understand this world; the good people are being killed by these **CRAZYS,** why?" I had no answer and none of the many TV contributors did either. Debbie loved Robert Kennedy he was her shining knight who was going to change the world for the better. His death really seemed to enlarge a crack in her. I began seeing and hearing her increasing frustrations with current political issues. I understood but I was so busy with my work and school at the time all I could do was verbally and emotionally support her.

I went up to Hooker, Oklahoma once that summer to check out how things were growing on Billy's farm and to see if I could estimate how much product we might end up with. It was awesome to view the plants in their natural habitat, in the ground, though they were hard to see between the rows of broom corn plants which were taller and more tightly packed. Both plants reached up toward the light. I still had no idea how much we would have to sell, but it was a sight to behold.

I had called Rudy first about my Broom pot and he agreed to follow me up to Oklahoma to buy the first thousand pounds at $60.00 per pound cash. That cash plus an additional $40,350 I brought paid for the 3, 345 pounds total that was harvested and which I bought that day.

I don't know how much he cleared on the broom corn that year, but he took home over a hundred thousand cash from me.

"Max," he told me," When I went into the bank president's office to pay off the whole note, the banker was smiling, assuming that the broom corn harvest was not going to cover the loan, so he was counting on making a big score off the farm. You should have seen the smile on that old son of a bitch's face drop and his mouth open when he looked into my dad's old leather briefcase and saw all those stacks of five thousand dollar bundles my mom had created. I was the talk of the town for quite a while though no one had any idea how we did it." Thank you again, Max, for your help." Then he grabbed my arm and shook my hand hard for quite a while before he gave me a really big Bear Hug, "I'll never forget this Max".

In less than three weeks I had most of my one hundred- thousand-dollar investment back with several more deliveries yet to make. My Oklahoma corn pot was the foot-in-the-door to start my wholesale business. I would soon have real working capital of $200,000 and could now move into the next phase of my plan. What I needed was a steady and reliable manufacturing source, the point of origin, for the constant band, which always had a demand and lots of cash in hand.

The next road trip to Houston was to be an important one for me on a couple of fronts. When I got to Dusty' s house, I was greeted warmly. This trip was my introduction to the world of psychedelics; I bought a few hits of acid and 6 peyote buttons and several mushrooms for myself and Debbie but did not try any until I was back in Denton. Dan explained that he had a friend at Rice University who ran the chemistry department where he was mixing the LSD as pure as it could be made by man. The mushrooms actually grew wild on cow manure in the pastures in the rural area just outside Houston. "On weekends, you'll find the old country roads with bumper-to-bumper traffic. People looking for a place to park so they can go on a trip in some good old boy's pasture," Dan laughed. "The peyote buds are easy to find, and they come from Mexico or West Texas that is if you know where to look; anyone can find them, or if you know how to ask the right people," He smirked.

Psychedelic drugs are very different from any other type of medication or recreational drugs. Psychedelic drugs change the brain's chemistry differently than it does with marijuana. One, Lysergic Acid Diethyl Amide, is better known as LSD, or Acid. This drug showed up in ancient times. It naturally developed from certain wheat grain under precise conditions in Israel. The grain had natural chemical reactions to the environment that it was stored in. We do not know whether the first documented manufacture of LSD was from an old formula or whether is it was just a quirk of nature, and all the needed elements came together with Mother Nature's tears to form LSD on the surface of this special grain which was made into bread by a religious sect in northern Israel. In any case, historians believe it was used to facilitate a religious experience or general enlightenment. The consumers of this bread went on a mind journey, either by accident or with expectation. It was found the same thing happened in Early American history, many believe it was the cause for the mass hysteria in Salem Massachusetts in the period from 1692 -1693, the Salem Witch Trials era.

This mind-altering drug changes the ordinary to the extraordinary. If you are tripping on acid and viewing the patterns on a couch, they will seem to expand, grow brighter, dance, or meld into new shapes. It brings introspection leading to self-discovery. It will open and alter your brain's perceptions. Even just one trip could change a person's life, opening them to totally different life choices.

The experiences of two Ph.D. professors at Harvard University exemplify this. One, Dr. Timothy Leary, a Psychology professor, was to become the spokesman for LSD experimentation. The other was Dr.

Richard Alpert who would morph into the enlightened Baba Ram Dass or "Servant of God." He writes of this transformation in the book,' *Be Here Now.*' Though they both took more than one trip on LSD, the first trip was the most important because it opened their minds to an alternative way of understanding. It was to be the first step in their individual life changing journeys. Acid or LSD also came to be known as the drug of "Sex, Drugs, and Rock-n-roll."

Psilocybin mushrooms provide a different high from acid or mescaline. It is a high as intense as marijuana but more expansive in a physical sense. Time has no boundaries. Sometimes a minute seems like hours; some hours seem to speed by in seconds. It is generally an intense high and can induce paranoia.

The most physically and mentally challenging high comes from mescaline, from the peyote bud of the mescal cactus. This is a very serious drug. The consumption of mescaline is like grabbing a tiger by the tail. You never know how it will grab you back or where it will drag you to. The high can be very intense, but the drug can also make you seriously physically sick and, if not prepared correctly, kill you.

When I returned from Dan's with the mind candy, I found Debbie was not home yet from her newest passionate cause. She was a founder of the Students for Democratic Society, or simply SDS. The group organized marches and promoted the occupation of several administrative buildings on university campuses across the country. They also participated in demonstrations and protested against the escalating war in Asia that the U.S. was involved in. Debbie and a few of her sisters from the N.O.W. group started an unofficial chapter here in Denton.

We decided to set aside a full day to try my new wares because we had no idea what to expect. Debbie was really excited about the "trip" we were about to take. She prepared our surroundings by lighting candles and incense and by placing every pillow in the house around us so that if we fell over, we would not hurt ourselves. Just watching her prepare was a trip in itself. We went on an LSD universe mind-journey for eighteen hours. Each of our experiences was different; we had no control over who went where.

Debbie's experience was sensual. She saw her viewpoint change and expand; she said later when we talked about this experience. "Max, I saw my role in the universe as a part of a bigger piece, almost like a cog in the wooden machine invented by Leonardo da Vinci. I do not remember what music was playing, though it sang to me, not in an audio way, but more like I was absorbing it through my skin." I think her trip was a cerebral one like looking through someone else's glasses.

My trip involved more visuals, more patterns, the furniture, the rugs, my shoes. All different colors, tones and textures that seemed to all belong together in some way. I had no appetite, and though our trips were different, we both felt that something opened up in our understanding of our world and lives.

A month later in May, Rodger and I cooked the tops of the peyote cactus buds. We boiled them in water for over three hours and then added sugar and grape Kool-Aid. The mescal buttons of the peyote cactus are sacred fruit to many in the Southwest. Mexicans and Native Americans have used this drug as a sacrament to the great spirits of the world; it is also a way to communicate with the dead and a gateway to another world or dimension.

The bud itself holds arsenic in the center of the fruit in the form of a fluffy white seed, somewhat like a dandelion flower. Also, the lower two-thirds of the bud are not used; only the top third which is a dark green and where the mind-altering chemicals reside. The dark green fruit is sliced into thinly cut buttons that are dried out in the sun. The consumer, most likely the Brujo, a sorcerer or medicine man, will chew fifteen to thirty of these dried buttons during the ancient ritual for their out-of-body journey.

Though Rodger and I did not prepare or consume our buds in the traditional way, our way produced intense results. The psychedelic experience of peyote is as much a physical trip as a mental one; with acid I did not become aware of my body as much. The more buttons consumed, the more intense the feeling and trip. The best way to describe it is a roller coaster ride. At first, the ride starts slowly. You feel yourself getting high, then a quick downward plummet. Each run up the tracks is higher and faster, but each downward run is likewise more intense. Nausea starts on the downward runs and even though the highs are awesome, the lows make you pay for this pleasure. When you puke, and you will, it feels like you are pushing all of your insides out your mouth. This happens several times and you have no control of your body or mind. The colors around the room became so intense that I wanted sunglasses to cut the brightness. Objects began to move. My TV screen began moving up and down the wall; my blue drapes were dancing with each other. The next experience I had was out-of- body. I found myself looking over a valley from a high mountain top, viewing downward. It was an incredible and beautiful sight, but I did not recognize it. I seemed comfortable and at home. The next thing I knew I was sitting in front of a very old man wearing rags. I'm trying to ask him questions, but all that came out of my mouth were garbled sounds, no words. The harder I tried to ask him my questions, the more the sounds coming out of my mouth were less like a language. The harder I tried to make him understand, the less I was able to communicate with him. It seemed very important for me to talk to this being. The old man just stared back at me with two warm, dark pools for eyes, as if he understood and cared. Then he started to giggle, which then turned into a deep belly laugh, and for some reason, that made me mad. Within a blink of an eye, he turned into a very scary monster that would pounce on me as if to devour me a little at a time. I was terrified, and my heart was beating like it was trying to pop out of my chest. I must have passed out because when I woke again, I found the floor covered in vomit and six hours had dissipated. I found Rodger in the back-yard, passed out with a mouth full of Bermuda grass. Thankfully, I had enough time to clean up the floors before Debbie got home. Afterward, I could understand how this could be interpreted as a religious experience by native peoples who had the ability to control where they went in the past, future or other time within the universe. There was something else I learned from my trip. This was not a drug I wished to try again.

In August of 68 Debbie's SDS Chapter traveled to Chicago to join the National Mobilization Committee to protest the War and they met up with another protesting the war group the Youth International Party, the YIPPIES. The groups were there to peacefully protest at the National Democratic Convention which was being held there. When over 10,000 people showed up to join in on the protest, Mayor Richard J. Daley, ordered 12,000 police officers along with 15,000 National Guardsmen to shut down the protesters. Things escalated quickly, and the police responded with tear gas and nightsticks. One girl in Debbie's group was beaten by a Chicago police officer and Debbie was arrested for disorderly conduct. My legal stick Abe got her out, but she was a charged lady when she did get back home.

"Max those sons of bitches were trying to hurt us. We came peacefully. Tom Hayden and Rennie Davis spoke of non-violence, using civil disobedience as our sword and for us to put up a united front. But they just kept charging and pushing. We had our right to be there and voice our opinions. Pushing became hitting. And the horses were used like we were the enemy. This is not right Max, and I'm going to do something about it."

"What can you do Debs?"

"I don't know yet, but …pass me that joint.

1969

The year 1969 was a year no one could ever forget. The west coast had the Haight Ashbury area of San Francisco which was the place to be if you were a free spirt looking for sex, drugs and the awesome rock- and -roll that came out of this place at that time. Though it was not quite as exciting as NASA's July 20 take-off and whose mission was to land on our very own Moon. This event was viewed by an estimate of up to 600,000,000 humans all looking up. We humans shared, through Neal Armstrong and Buzz Aldrin, a monumental moment in time. With Armstrong's, "one small step," we had done a giant leap for mankind." We all had walked on the moon.

While the Haight was the cool place to be on the West Coast in 1969, Max Yasgur's farm in White Lake, New York was the other place to be, on the East Coast. During weekend of August 15-17 approximately half a million people showed up to a musical fair, The Woodstock Music & Art Fair, forever after known as simply "Woodstock." The promoters promised "peace, music, and co-existence." Tickets were priced seven dollars for one day, thirteen for two days; eighteen dollars got attendees a full three-day pass. If they got lucky, the promoters hoped to sell twenty thousand to twenty-five. They got very lucky indeed. One hundred eighty-six thousand tickets were presold, but after the first day when several hundred thousand more people showed up without tickets, the promoters were unable to control the arriving masses so decided to open the concert for free admittance.

The first time in known history that almost a half-a- million people showed up, in one location. At the same time, it is not for a military encounter (war) but for a peace-loving event.

The music line up would include some of the greatest musical talent of the '60s. Legendary performers such as Jimmy Hendrix and Janis Joplin were just two of the preeminent musicians that emerged from the depths of the entertainment pool. A confluence of rock, country, blues, soul and folk singers, - never before had there been so much talent in one spot, at one time, live-in front of an audience of over 400,000.

Food, drinking water and clean restrooms were in short supply. Mother Nature provided lots of rain and lots of sunshine. Several babies were born during the event. Despite all the problems, Woodstock had very little crime. There was also a lot of marijuana smoke coming off those hills, the largest smoke-in ever. Many believe it helped keep the peace and harmony of this temporary city.

October of 69 brought over 1 million protesters to Washington D.C. to rally against the Asia conflicts. The meeting of the protesters was to be at the Lincoln Memorial but with the unexpected numbers, the sea of people filled the entire mall.

Just after Christmas I bought airline tickets for Debbie, Rodger, his girlfriend and myself, as a splurge trip, to Acapulco for a few days of sand, sun and fun. When I bought the LSD from Dusty, he showed me how to take blotter paper and a hole puncher and with an eye dropper, make dot acid to sell the acid by the dot. I carried some with me to sell to students in the area. On the second day, while the girls and Rodger went shopping for silver jewelry, Mexican blankets, pots, and puppets for their families, I went back to the old cantina to find Juan and renew our friendship. Our business in the past had been profitable for both of us. Unfortunately for me, he had moved back to Puerto Rico with his family. I managed to sell some of my blotter acid to a couple of college students from Pittsburgh and another group from France.

On the last day of our four-day visit, I went back to Playa Puerto beach to peddle some more of these dots to anyone interested, college kids or not. I was talking to a couple of kitchen workers from my hotel and was about to make my pitch when another of their friends joined the group. He was about twenty-five years old and looked overdressed in a white Guayabera shirt and dark slacks. He asked if I had something to sell. The hair on the back of my neck jumped up; I sensed this was not going to go well. "Senor, what do you have to sell?" He reached over and stuck his fingers in my shirt pocket, pulling out the LSD dots.

I attempted to explicate myself but the man now holding my acid proved to be a Mexican Federal Police officer. Before I could say anything, he had me in handcuffs. I was arrested right there and then. No Miranda, no innocent until otherwise proven; he didn't care about what I had to say. The two hotel employees were gone when I looked up. I was not beaten but handled roughly, and those big, burly men sure scared the shit out of me. I was taken to a very old building in downtown Acapulco. The outside of the building was freshly whitewashed stucco, but the inside was filthy. It looked like it hadn't seen a cleaning since the place first opened up. The walls were dark from smoke and dust, the holding cell where I was deposited had light only from a small, barred window and a single lightbulb fixture high above the floor. The smell of unwashed bodies along with the other stench of other bodily fluids nauseated me. The five beds were occupied. I found a small space by the piss-and-shit bucket. In the meantime, the police had found my room key and had gone to my hotel room and searched for it thoroughly. The *Federaliies' found* nothing, thank God. They made sure the rest of my group left on the next flight back to Dallas. I was able to receive a short call from Debbie before she left. "Look Deb, there is nothing you can do for me now, so go home. Contact my folks and advise them that I'll try to get in touch as soon as I can." What else could any of us do?

I spent three frustrating days in this cell before I was even questioned, with nothing to do but think. Think about my stupid choice to sell LSD. Think about what Debbie will do. Think about my family's reaction. Think about school. Think about spending the rest of my days in this god-forsaken rat pen. Two of my cell mates, locals, were pretty good guys, they filled me in as to what to expect from the Mexican legal system. "The key to your problems, my friend, can be solved with cash," was Stefano's advice. "Yes, cash solves many legal problems here in Mexico."

On the third day of my incarceration, a Federali Police officer requested my company. I had not yet showered, changed clothes or even shaved, and I had not eaten much. I was taken to the office of one Lieutenant Antonio Gutrez, a young Castilian with dark brown eyes and fair skin. "Mr. Gold, it is against the law to possess or sell psychedelic drugs in Mexico, and since you were arrested with illegal drugs in the act of trying to distribute said illegal drugs, you will be brought in front of a judge in a few months. You can expect about a ten-year sentence for breaking the Federal Mexican drug laws. Even if you do have a good American attorney, you will need a very good and expensive Mexican one. And yes, you were guilty were you not, Mr. Gold," he asked.

My heart was doing roller coaster dives, beating out of my chest. As prompted by my new friend, I deicide to double down and asked, "Lieutenant, sir, I was wondering if a financial solution might be arranged to avoid costly and valuable court time?" What seemed like minutes passed and I could hardly breathe. I felt like a spring wound too tight and about to break.

Gutrez looked me squarely in the eyes. Then with an ever-so-serious look he replied," Are you trying to bribe me, gringo?"

"Oh no, sir," I quickly replied. "It just seems that an arrangement could be reached that could benefit both of us."

He just stared at me, his face grim, and then finally said, "Perhaps."

I breathed out in relief now knowing it was just a matter of negotiating a price. Lieutenant Gutrez started at one hundred thousand American dollars, but I got him down to thirty-five thousand in U.S. cash, a donation to him and his associates. The rest was just logistics. I was able to use the phone in the Lieutenant's office to call my dad back in Dallas. He was the only one I knew who would and could bail me out of this debacle.

This was not a call I wanted to make but I really had no other choice. Dread hung in my mind as I dialed those numbers on the old rotary phone. I knew my folks would bail me out but the disappointment I knew they would feel also covered me with additional guilt. "Hello," answered my mother.

"Hello, Mom, I'm really sorry I have put you all through this and…"

"Max, are you all, right? Are you hurt? What can we do for you, Max? How can we help?" All this came rushing out of my mom's mouth at lightning speed.

I pushed back my strong feelings and said softly, "I'm okay, Mom, really, but I need to talk to Dad.

When Harold came on the phone it was all business. He did not give me time to say anything before he asked, "How much money do you need Max, any particular denominations? Where? I'll be there as soon as I can." He was in Gutrez's office in less than twenty-four hours, cash in hand. He had gotten a personal loan for $35,000 from his credit union. Those twenty-four hours of waiting afforded me time to evaluate the situation, knowing I was not going to prison in Mexico just yet. Inspired by listening to my new "roommates" and as they had enlightened me with their personal experiences. I got an idea, **"To achieve great things,**

two things are needed; a plan, and not quite enough time." Money caused my present situation, so maybe more money might solve my new supply needs.

Deal done and alone with Gutrez, I got a stern warning about coming back to Mexico.

I took a deep breath, reevaluated the risk for a short min- second and jumped in., "Since we have such a good working relationship now Lieutenant, how about continuing it? Let me purchase my Mexican marijuana from you directly in more U.S. currency." It was a 50/50 gamble. I was betting on all this cash was going to make him hungrier for more.

"How are you going to get it across the border?" He questioned.

"Well, sir, I don't know yet, but if you can supply me with enough kilos or pounds of marijuana at a reasonable price and assure my safety to the border, I will do the rest." Although his face appeared contemplative, his eyes were already saying, "Yes, we have a deal. "He pulled out his business card which already had his private phone home number written neatly on the back.

"Call me in a couple of months. We will work out the details. I assume you have the *cohunes'* needed for this size venture, Mr. Gold." I was not sure if he was talking about cash for the buy or the size of my nuts or the wherewithal to pull this off.

I knew I was taking a substantial risk. I could get ripped off; I could get busted; I could get robbed; I could get killed. However, my gut told me this was a good move. I also knew that this was too good an opportunity to pass up as the Lieutenant had put his phone number on the back of the card before I had made my move. All his drama was just a way to squeeze me and make me pay my dues. Making just one or two bountiful trips over the border would be less risky than making multiple drug runs with small quantities. Now all I had to do was to come up with a plan. *HOW?*

My jubilation was quickly tempered on the return trip to Dallas and the good old U.S.A. as my seat mate was my dad. The trip home with Harold was, to say the least, rather chilly. In the beginning, all he said was, "Max I am very disappointed in you." His words stung, as they were meant to. Over the years Harold had actually spent more time with my older brother Danny. They shared an interest in electronics these days as they had, years earlier, in an electric train set that I had not been allowed to touch or play with. It had taken up an ample portion of our garage with a layout that included small towns and farms, incorporating tiny houses, cars, trees, billboards and people along and inside of the twisting oval train tracks. Harold and Danny would spend hours working on that thing together, excluding me. I hated that train set. On the other hand, my dad was no longer close to my sister. Judy had developed physically too soon for Harold, and when he no longer had a little girl, he quit hugging her or tickling her, something that they had enjoyed when she was younger. My role was to be the son who took over the store and continued the Gold dynasty. All I got were more words of wisdom as business advice from Harold, in an attempt to forge a relationship with me through work. I guess he thought this was the only thing we had in common. I broke the tension shortly after takeoff I wanted to explain, as best as I could, what I had been up to and why I had been caught. I did not follow my own rules. Look Pop, I'm sorry I got you and Mom involved in this at all; I'll have the money back to you before the end of the week, I wanted to promise him. Dad, I am done with that life. Ect ect bull shit. But what I really, really wanted to explain, that some people buy music, and others are born to write it and play it. My thing was to sell it, spread the message, to be the Johnny Appleseed of the cannabis plant. Of course, neither of those things was said. Because no sooner had I said" Look Pop," He cut me off with.

"Max, you are a smart guy. You could put some energy into work on something legal. Why take such stupid risks? Just for money? It can't end well son. But I know you well enough that you have already made your mind up but know this. Although we do love you, Max, this is the last time I will bail you out. Understand you can't put your mother through all this tzurace again (grief, or aggravation, headaches)."

I had the taste of excitement, the adventure of the deal, the unbelievable profit for time spent. My course was set, if I had of been born in the 1600's maybe I would have been a trader sailing the Seven Seas trading spices, jewels, drugs, who knows, but I was here and now. The marijuana business was where the opportunity and excitement could be found for me.

Back in Denton, I was warmly greeted by Debbie whose first words were, "Max, how much did that cost you? You did make a pay-off, right?

What you're not glad to see me?"

"No, it is just that there are two systems out there, one for the poor, every day and one for the ones with money."

"The golden rule my dear" as Zady loved to say**," He who has the gold, Rules."** "Besides Ms. Cooper I don't remember you complaining when Abe bailed you out in Chicago. With no response from Debbie, I continued. "On the good news side, we now have a great, steady, dependable, and most importantly the safe source of Senorita Marijuana." I gave her a short version of the past several days. "I just need to work out the small details, like how I'm going to get it across. I'm sure not going to do what I did last time." I also was going to have to hustle to get more working capital after I paid my folks back.

1970

Jimi Hendrix dies of an overdose of barbiturates on September 18, while living in London, then just a few weeks later on October 4, Janis Joplin died of an overdose of heroin, alone in a cheap hotel in Hollywood.

*President Richard Nixon signed off on the "Drug Abuse Prevention and Control Act of 1970." This was to be a comprehensive federal war on drugs, but its real purpose was to target marijuana smokers in additional to more serious drug users. Supported by the invisible **"silent majority,"** who blamed **Hippies** and their drug culture for the political unrest.*

In early March I contacted Lieutenant Gutrez by phone, dialing the number written on the back of his card. He promptly answered, "Captain Gutrez." I guess he had used some of my "donation" to procure a promotion. "I have all you can use, Mr. Gold. How much can you handle?" He was anxious to do more cash business. I would need to be where he directed me within forty-eight hours or less, if possible. We haggled over his demanding price. I agreed to buy four thousand pounds at thirty-five dollars per pound. "Senor Gold, you purchase will be ready for pick up by the end of August or the beginning of September, so have my cash ready."

"He must be eyeing his boss' job," I thought to myself.

I felt good about the call. If he was just going to rip me off, he would have tried to get me to come down sooner. Six months gave me the time I needed to learn to pilot an airplane.

It had always been a dream of mine to learn to fly. I now had a real need to learn. I checked out a couple of flight schools in the area. At the first one, Bob of Bob's School of Flight, asked too many questions, but the second was run by an ex-Vietnam War veteran, an Air Force pilot who had flown over one hundred missions during his tour of duty. Chuck McCullum and I hit it off right from the start. He seemed to sense what I was up to, but never once asked. He would, as we spent more and more time together in the small two-seater, tell me of his flying experiences, giving me tips for unforeseen circumstances. Your average pilot would not need to know a few of these circumstances. "Max," he said one late afternoon just before sundown as we were practicing nighttime flying, taking off and landing in the dark, "I want you to know how to fly at night using land references and how to fly under the radar, so to speak." From that session on a lot of my training seemed to be customized for the special type of flying I was going to do which would include a lot of dirt runway landings in the little out-of-the way rural airports. My least favorite flying was in bad weather. I did not like feeling like a feather in a wind or rainstorm.

After I had completed the necessary flight hours and had passed the entire physical and written test, I got my license. I was ready for Part B of my big plans. The border areas of Texas, New Mexico, and Arizona are huge with many flight routes to choose from. At the time much of this massive area was not under surveillance by any authorities, but likewise it is not ideal for a small plane to just drop down and land. Rodger and I spent a lot of time looking over maps, and airtime canvassing those areas chosen for potential landing and loading sites. We found that there were lots of large ranches in these spaces and some had good roads. We would locate several in the air then go back in a truck to see things from the ground to check out access and egress. The ideal location needed to be out of the way with good roads, or at least flat land free of large rocks and smooth enough not to tear up the plane as it landed. By the end of the summer, we had picked out four sites that would give us good landings and take-offs, plus easy access to the county roads. We spent enough time in the areas familiarizing ourselves, so we would not get lost by day or night on these back roads of Texas.

I slowly added more clients and other dealers to my list of wholesale buyers. I would not sell for less than twenty-five pounds, but most of my buyers bought at least fifty pounds at a time, and several were big enough to buy in hundreds of pounds quantities.

Rodger was enrolled at NT, and through him, I met one of his classmates, one "Vinny" Gambo. Vincent was from Brooklyn, Neeew Yaaarrk, and had come to North Texas State to study jazz; his instrument was the saxophone. Vinny was what you would have expected; a loud, boisterous know-it-all. He told Rodger and I, that his family was connected to a well-known mobster gang. I did not care about his family ties as long as he had the cash and Rodger OK'd him. He bought twenty-five pounds initially. It turned out he was a steady customer for us; whenever he returned home, he always took at least one hundred pounds or more of our product.

The funny thing about most of these guys that came to Denton from the Northeast is they would do nothing but talk about how great it was back home, wherever that was. After being on campus for a few months, they went home to visit the old neighborhood. Amazingly, when they returned to school, you seldom again heard how great it was back at their home. This happened more often than not. I finally came to the conclusion that, after just a few months of living in Texas, these guys had found the warm, friendly, trusting people here more open and laid-back. In Texas the old Southern culture of common courtesy, manners and hospitality meets the Old West. Back home did not seem quite as great in comparison. On weekends Vinny played at a jazz club in south Dallas. A group of Vinny, Cleo and his cousin Dewayne were waiting for me one afternoon when I came to make my delivery to Vinny at his house.

"Max, this is my buddy, Cleo Washington. I told him you could hook him up, huh! "

He had Cleo, his boss, the club owner and Cleo's cousin, to the drop. Vinny had not asked me if I would be interested in meeting this small-time dealer who wanted to get bigger. I do not like surprises, so I had but two choices leave or stay and do business. My gut did not give off any negative vibes, so I decided to stay.

"Nice to meet you, Brother," I said. He seemed to have lots of cash and was ready to spend some with me. He started buying twenty-five pounds minimum per month in addition to buying lots of Dan's products. His partner was his cousin Dewayne. They were flashy guys, lots of gold, expensive alligator shoes, custom clothes in bright colors, and enough bling on their fingers and neck to open a new Zales. One of my stipulations in selling to the Flash Brothers was that they had to tone down their auto, clothes, silver and gold jewelry when we did business. That included foregoing Cleo's custom Lime Green Caddy. We found that if we did our business in an old church parking lot just after services started, we could easily see any activity in the area plus nobody paid any attention to us.

Just that easily, I grew my business, moving more and more tonnage. I was so busy with making preparations for the picking up of new products, the delivery of said product and keeping proper business records that I must admit I had not figured out how to pay my taxes.

Also, I was thus my classwork was suffering short on time with all the new traveling I was doing. I was always tired and. I knew I could not drop out, or I would be wearing Army green instead of smoking it.

Over the next few months since we had gotten back from Mexico, Debbie slowed down selling and in fact hardly hung out with her old cronies. Her new cohorts were more radical, who talked of blowing stuff up to get the class war started right here in the USA. "Bring the troops home and let's get this country straightened out once and for all!"

After just one session of that at the house I said, "No more." That brought Debbie and me into a full-face screaming match. I did not want any of this group back in our home if for no other reason I did not need any crazies, to bring attention to me now. In the end we agreed to disagree. But she agreed it would not be wise to bring any of them back around me.

In late May through early June at Kent State University students struck daily, to protest the increased bombing in Cambodia. After a ROTC building was set on fire the Governor called in the Ohio National Guard to maintain order and stop the spread of these protests. These weekend warriors were armed with M1 rifles with bayonets and live ammunition. Their training was for war, not for herding college students. Of the seventy-seven-armed National Guardsmen, 29 shot at least one shot. The total 66 shots were fired resulting in four students being killed and nine more wounded. This triggered millions of protesters on over 450 college campuses across the nation, and it brought consequences to my life I was not expecting.

Shortly after the Kent State massacre, Debbie dropped out of school and out of my life. Her parting words were, **"I love you Max, but this is bigger than us playing house. They are out to kill us and I'm going to fight back."** Poof like that she left with a small backpack and was gone.

"I love you Max, but..." is all I remember. It was as if someone had hit me in the stomach with a baseball bat. I could not have been more deflated. I had a hard time breathing, and by the time I got to the front door and outside she was gone. All I had left were the whys and what ifs. Answers I knew somehow, I would not find answers to at least anytime soon.

In 1966 when I began this part of my life as caretaker, nurture and number one fan of Cannabis and all her fine properties I was just trying to spread the word through friends, classmates, mostly college-educated people who had as much to risk if police were to become involved as I did, but as time moved on I was now dealing with friends of friends, and friends of, just put me one or two step further away from the inside source, my friend. People were getting busted more often, taking a plea giving up everyone they knew. My own paranoia began wearing me down. If the buyer was freaked out or nervous, it would put me on high alert. I was also to find out as time went by. I was the dealer friend not a friend who was a dealer, a big difference. I was hoping the change from retail to wholesale would help. Fewer people, less exposure, more product. Which would bring its own set of worries? Large amounts of grass meant a larger footprint for bulks storage of the tonnage. Then the other big worry is, it's by-product, **"CASH"**, which would also attract less desirables, the low lifers looking for an easy score. The stress of the business was slowly taking the joy of the deal, replacing it with anxiety.

I decided not to go to summer school in the summer of 1970, but I had pre-registered for the fall semester, so I would not have the draft board on my neck. Through some screw up, the University had failed to notify my draft board of my pre-registration for the fall classes, so in June I got a notice from the Dallas board informing me that my student status had been changed to I-A, making me eligible for the draft. Two days later I got my personal invitation to join the doctors in downtown Dallas for my pre-induction physical. I was to show up at four o'clock a.m. I got copies of my student records from the Registration Office at UNT to take with me. The Army personnel were not sympathetic when I reported as ordered and tried to show my paperwork to explain the obvious mistake in my receiving the summons. "It will be worked out later," said the old Sargent.

The inspection was done by very stern military personnel who were not taking any crap from anyone. Thirty-two other naked men and I were thoroughly examined from the top of our heads to the bottom of our feet and everywhere in between. I had thought that the experience in the Mexican jail was humiliating, but this was even worse. We were told to "Turn your head and cough" while some other guy fondled the family jewels. I need to say no more.

At one point we were told to bend over and spread our cheeks in preparation for a minimally lubricated, gloved finger to exam our rectums in full view of all the other guys. One unfortunate dude was not given an opportunity to use the restroom before his exam. After the doctor pulled out a shit-covered finger from his ass, he demanded, "What the hell is this?"

"It isn't peanut butter, mister," the wise guy answered. It broke us all up. Though the lieutenant's face turned bright red, he could not do much about it, yet. During the next couple of hours, we were given a battery of written exams with a jillion question. "Do you sleepwalk? Do you wet the bed? Are you a homosexual? Do you hate you mother?" There was a small group of five guys who must have been friends enlisting together through the buddy system. They were all gung-ho and braggadocios about how they were going to kill a bunch of Commie Gooks. Little did they realize that the people they would be facing had more to win than we did and were willing to lose more to accomplish their goals? These guys had no idea what really awaited them when they faced the enemy on the other side of the world. For two thousand years this culture and its people had fought off the invading armies of Chinese, Japanese, English, and French for decades and had defeated them all.

I finally got to the end of the line only to see the administrative sergeant. I showed him my paperwork from school. He just smiled and said, "I'll see you back here next year after graduation." By the time I got home to Denton, I was worn-out and in much need of a really big Dobie.

I had a renewed motivation not to drop out of school now for sure. And I had a very short time to move four thousand pounds of product that I had made a commitment to buy from Guterz. For the fall semester I registered for twelve credit hours, the minimum required to qualify as a full-time student to give myself more time to travel yet still keep the draft board at bay.

Just before Labor Day 1970, I flew into Mexico in a leased a Beechcraft Musketeer to fly in my first shipment of Mexican pot from Captain Guterz. As I had rented this type of plane from the same small airport for several months as we were searching for safe crossing and landing sites, the two airport employees were used to seeing Rodger and I sporadically coming and going. To my growing assets, I added a used one-ton Ford pickup with auxiliary fuel tanks loaded with airplane-grade fuel for refueling the plane. We used a deserted ranch outside Del Rio, Texas, for our first meet-up to unload. Rodger kept a few small fires lit and fed along the landing road so I could see where to land. Three plane loads with no more than five hundred pounds each load would fit into the camper I had added to the bed of the Ford to blend in with the rest of the good Ol', country folks.

The first solo crossing of the Rio Grande was ass tightening and exhilarating both. I was faced with a real challenge head-on with enthusiasm and it was another personal challenge for me.

I had the readings as to where to be and when and as I approached the location I could see looking down, that on one end of the highway were police cars stopping traffic and on the other far end another group one with a truck and a black sedan also holding traffic. The landing could not been any easier, and I had no sooner come to a full stop and stepped out of the plane when my new best friend Captain Guterz showed up in a new black Ford sedan, he checks the cash while I check the pot. "This Mister Gold is from Oaxaca, the best I should get more for this premium product."

"This may indeed be the great product you exalt; we will be doing lots of business in the future; this is just a small taste of what money we can make for each other, eh?" By the third trip I had paid Guterz $46,690 for 1334 total pounds.

As Rodger and I were driving back to Austin, it being our first stop, it dawned on me, "I am the guy that people are waiting for. **The Man, the Guy, the Dude.**" The guy, who so many times before. That I had waited on, and it only had just been a few short blips of time ago.

Rudy had an amazing old warehouse that was in a rural, undeveloped part of Austin, mostly Hispanic. Rudy bought one thousand pounds of this first load. The rest I had committed to another couple of people, at seventy-five dollars a pound. Juan's business was expanding faster than mine, and his brother Arturo was now making the smaller drops as Juan used to do with me. "Rudy, are you guys still getting most of your stuff across by way of family and friends via mules?" I asked as we sat in his comfortable office, smoking some of our newest acquisitions.

"Fuoooo," he blew out the smoke, leaned back, smiled. "Max, my family has been in the smuggling business for many years. I've told you before we do have friends, family and employees who come across every day, and have years, to work in Laredo and I guess you could call them mules. Each person will bring across as little as a pound up to fifteen or more at a time. Not every day, but often enough to bring in at least a couple hundred pounds a week. The rest I buy from different dumb-ass gringos like you two." I asked him about his cousin Crystal. "My uncle now has a flesh and blood son-in-law, but he still uses the vibrator when he is by himself watching football on TV."

I flew back to Mexico the following weekend and repeated the process, flying into Mexico only landing back in Texas at a different ranch. Each trip was easier than the previous one. By the end of October 1970, I had sold over three thousand pounds and still had eight hundred seventy-five pounds to sell. By the end of the season, Ol' MM had grossed almost $400,000. I could have bumped up my game and brought in more people to sell, but Rodger and I had discussed this in depth. Separately, using Ben Franklin's decision-making process, we each made one Pros vs. Cons list, compared them and concluded that our current risk was manageable. The more people we involved, the more the risk would expediently grow. In the end it boiled down to we trusted each other, so no add-ons for this private company.

All in all, I was very happy with this year's business and as my business grew, so would my ties to Mexico grow. I thought of becoming a farmer and growing my own, but I was not patient enough to watch it grow slowly. Mexico was my answer.

During the rest of the year, I made trips to Houston to visit Dusty and returned with Mary Jane from around the world some of which I sold to the sales reps at the men's and women's wear shows. Dusty always had stock no one else might have in this part of the world, so when I told Mr. Lenny Putz that his quarter of an ounce from the jungles of India would cost $500, he couldn't get the cash out of his pocket fast enough. Sorry Lenny, no checks. Even some of my regular wholesale customers would always pay up for some exotic weed. Selling this premium-grade cannabis was my greatest joy. This was more than a business. Through a shared appreciation of this holy plant while passing joints and sharing stories, we develop a unique comradery, Brothers of Smoke. Social drinking is more of an individual sport, one which often stymies conversation and there is no sense of community. But when you share the smoke, you share an existential pleasure by literally sharing a joint, bong, or pipe, **United in Smoke**. Therein lies the crucial difference between drinking and smoking.

I have always been very conservative, never flamboyant or flashy. I did not buy a new set of wheels or any glitzy gold jewelry with my new cash. I paid myself a yearly salary of $100,000 plus bonuses which I took in gold. This is America after all, home of the brave… and the capitalist. The cash went into safety deposit boxes in three different banks.

I could have graduated at the end of spring semester 1970, if I had taken a full load, but the draft board was waiting for me. Having already passed the pre-induction exams, I would be in boot camp by the end of June. I decided to attend school, again taking a minimum of twelve hours, then to go to graduate school until the war ended. I was becoming a highly educated dealer of *Marijuana*.

Every one of my clients increased their orders, but when I called the newly promoted Colonel Gutrez to place next year's order, his price had increased from thirty-five to fifty dollars a pound. We went through the bargaining dance until we agreed on forty-three dollars. My order was a five-ton minimum. I called on David McCullum, my old flight teacher, and made him an offer. It only took him three seconds to reply, "I was hoping to hear from you. Yes, let's do this." He would fly a twin-engine plane while I flew the single engine. We could bring in about two thousand pounds a trip, less exposure. My drive to South Texas and back to Denton was taking longer because I was now pulling a slower but safer twin-axel cargo trailer. Again, most of the inventory was sold in the first six days. I kept 2,000 pounds to use to fill the summer demand from my regulars before the new harvest came. I could charge an additional fifteen to twenty percent for the same product I had sold a few months earlier because of the shortage of available product during these months. Simply put supply and demand. If there is more demand for a limited supply, the price rises. But even that ton of pot did not last long. The U.S. Government had started to pressure the Mexican government to halt the growing and trafficking of my bread and butter. Joint task forces of the Mexican and American militaries sprayed liquid defoliate on many, many thousands of acres of prime green marijuana. The heat was on.

"Hola, Colonel, I greeted him. How are you and your family doing?"

"Senior Gold how is it you always seem to know when to call? Do you have one of my men on your payroll?" he chuckled. "I was going to call you anyway. How soon can you pick up a load? My men have stopped a truck in Cananea with five hundred fifty-five kilos of your cargo. I need to either bring it in and report it or if you can pick it up within the next twenty-four hours, you can have it for $90 a kilo."

"Who do I make the check-out to?" no second-guessing that decision.

By the time I came back from visiting one of my safety deposit boxes at the bank, Rodger had gotten a lead from one of our friends at the small airport we sometimes used in South Texas near Del Rio when bad weather conditions forced us to change plans. Jim, the owner-operator, charges by the load of counter- ban, no haggling. It was Jim's runway, so his way. The main business for El Frido airport was crop dusting. So, the extra cash they occasionally received from types like me really helped their bottom line. I rented a plane in Tucson and made my short flight to the border town's rural airport.

Rodger met me at the small airport where we unloaded the rear and front passenger seats. As I flew in over the airport to land, I noticed a box truck parked behind the small office building. Did someone seem to be waiting inside the truck? "Rodger, after I leave, go over and check the guy in the truck, and let me know by blinking your head lights if it's okay to land." I did not want to fly back into a bust.

In the airport office Rodger checked with our guy, Don, the manager there, and learned that the truck driver had been there for almost a full day, waiting for a Mexican shipment. "Like you guys, he comes a couple times a year. I think he comes from Phoenix." When Rodger left the office, he headed straight to the box truck, engaging the driver in conversation. Within just a few minutes they were sharing a joint. The driver was not a cop. Evan Burk was his name, a manager of an exclusive golf and tennis county club in Phoenix. He also sold a lot of Mary Jane to his members. "I had watched you and the pilot unloading the seats from of your plane and put two and two together. Most of my business is retail, but I do sell some weight to a couple of people in the area. My suppliers have a tunnel out there somewhere nearby because they always want to meet here.

"Sooo, how long have you been waiting for your delivery, Evan?" Rodger coughed out as he took another hit and passed the joint.

"I've been here… too many…hours," he spat out between coughing fits. "This is some nasty shit you got here Roger. Wooooo! I am feeling nothing. My whole body is numb."

"Yea, it's from Afghanistan, some backward Arab country that grows this very sticky cannabis plant, it is what they use to make primo hash," tells Rodger.

"Oooooh, I haaave had only had to wait thiiiisss long once befooore." Silence ruled for the next half hour as we drifted into our separate nirvanas. When the conversation returned, Evan explained that his suppliers had a tunnel out there somewhere.

Rodger muttered, "How much are you paying per pound?"

"One hundred dollars a pound."

Rodger thought to himself, "It's probably more likely one ten to one hundred thirty per pound."

"Evan buddy, I have to tell you, there is a very good chance that your guys will not show up. If you want to wait that's okay, but MM can probably work you a deal on this stuff he is bringing in now. How much are you looking to purchase?"

"Well, I was expecting 1,500 pounds or so," Evan responded.

The tunnel Evan had referred to turned out to be twenty feet deep. A light gauge rail track had been built inside the tunnel on which small carts filled with marijuana, other drugs and contraband. The freight was pulled by winches. I was sure someone was making a killing. This was just one of hundreds of similar large drug-smuggling operations, working twenty-four hours a day, seven days a week up and down the border, Texas to California. All this inside information came to me while watching Walter Cronkite report the details of the operation and of the tunnel which a Mexican- U.S. combined task force had raided and shut-down. The Government has to score a victory every once in a while. **"Even a blind squirrel can find a nut every once in a while."**

When I made my fly-by and Rodger turned the truck lights, I landed we had a short verbal exchange. Rodger told me about his conversation with Evan, so I went over to and introduced myself as MM from Dallas. We made a deal for $110 per pound; he would buy the entire load. Rodger, Evan, and I unloaded the first haul. They tallied and weighed some of the bundles as I left for the next load. I was back in seventy-five minutes.

1971

Postage stamps are eight cents; a movie ticket is $1.50, gas forty cents a gallon.

United Parcel Service began to complete with United States Post Office for the package delivery business.

Cigarette advertising is banned on TV and Mick Jagger and Keith Richards are sentenced on marijuana drug charges.

The Harris Poll of public opinion showed 60% of Americans are against the war in Vietnam.

Inflation is out of control and President Nixon implements a 90-day wage and price freeze.

1972

The last American ground troops leave Viet Nam.

President Richard Nixon visits China.

16 people are rescued from a plane crash site, where they had survived by cannibalism.

ERA passed the Senate.

The Summer Olympics held in Munich was interrupted by eight heavily armed members of the Terrorists group Black September who broke in the Israeli athletics' quarters at the Village. Their demands were for a swap and release of 232 Palestinians being held in prison. After a botched rescued attempt, the count ended with eleven Israeli Team members, five Terrorists and one police officer all dead.

WATERGATE TIMELINE

"There is no proxy in transgression"

June 13, 1971 the Watergate disaster started with former defenses analyst, Dr. Daniel Ellsberg leaking the "Pentagon Papers", to the national news. These were to reveal the true secret history behind the Vietnam War. The New York Times begins publishing section of these papers showing how the American government had been lying to the American people about this war.

September 3, 1971, brought national attention to the Republican's plumbers', a unit that broke into Ellsberg's office to find the leak.

June 17, 1972, the same group of men was discovered burgling the offices of the National Democratic Committee, at the Watergate Hotel complex in Washington D.C.

The drama of the events would lead to the discovery that these men were sent by high-ranking Republicans in the Nixon administration. President Nixon had tape recordings of meetings about these events and of his involvement in the subsequent cover-up attempt.

Even after the joint houses of Congress requested the full release of all tapes to be reviewed, and after all his legal maneuvering did not work and the Supreme Court issued orders for the release. The President refused.

July 27, 1974 the House of Representatives' Judiciary Committee passed the first of three articles of impeachment.

On Augusts 8, 1974 President Richard M. Nixon resigned.

As a good citizen, I too decided to keep my prices the same as last year's from $ 110 to $180 a pound, depending on how much you bought.

Two weeks after graduation, I got a call from Vinny Gambo, Rodger's New York friend. I recognized his nasal voice immediately. He said, "We need to talk **ASAP**. It's important."

"Meet me at the truck stop in fifteen," I answered, but from his voice I knew some was wrong. I had only been sitting in the booth for a few minutes when Vinny showed up and sat across from me, ordered his coffee and then turned his attention back to me.

"Cleo was busted last night by undercover Dallas Police officers at the Black Horse for selling coke, and I don't trust that ass not to roll over on us all for a reduced sentence. You've been supplying him the pot. I have been supplying him with coke, but they will be looking for both of us, if I know how the police work and Cleo's character. I'll get this handled, don't woorry," Vinny said reassuringly. "Yoou just need to lay low for a while. It may take a little time, but as long they cannot find yoou, they can't serve the warrant on youss."

I had been dreading this day for more than one reason. I went home and contacted Rodger to let him know what was up and for him to lay low as well. I left the truck in my driveway after it was cleaned out, and Rodger dropped me off at the airport. I made one last call to "Abe, the Barbarian," my lawyer, to give him a heads up.

"Max," he responded, "Stay close but invisible. I'll check and see what I can find out."

I did not go too far. In a cheap Rent-A-Wreck I drove to a small area lake and rented an old Airstream trailer and a small wooden rowboat so I could pass the time by fishing.

As Vinny had predicted, four days after I left, the Denton Police and a DEA agent by the name of Dwight Longstead came with a warrant to search my home. They really tore the place up as I would find later. Though they did not find anything in the house or the truck, they impounded my truck anyway. I checked with Vinny every few weeks, and just took it easy, read a lot, fished and stayed out of sight.

This downtime allowed me to do some future planning. I had not paid any income tax in several years, and I knew that when this legal problem was resolved, I would need to set myself up in a legal business. For fun Debbie and I went to estates sales and occasionally traveled to the little town of Canton in East Texas for Trade Days. The first Monday of every month actually begins the preceding weekend, bringing in farmers with produce, livestock, antiques, pets, and anything else that the area people wanted to sell. The First Monday Trade Days have been held for almost a hundred years. There were always interesting things to buy at bargain prices; then it's always fun to look at other people's junk. I had furnished my house in Denton with a lot of old wood furniture from the '20s through the '50s. Though not really antiques, they were well-built wooden pieces. It seemed that people were just starting to appreciate older craftsmanship.

This might be a good cover business; I could pay cash for some of the purchases and run some of my "dirty money" through the business if I was careful. Cash is always great, but I would need to establish lines of credit and have legal money to pay for personal and business expenses. This way I would have a way to show how I was making a living and a way to pay some taxes. I knew I wanted to buy a home, and I needed to have good credit and the ability to show a steady income. The federal government was making it harder to deposit large amounts of cash into bank accounts without sending up smoke signals. All in all, this seemed to be a good place to start my new career as an independent, legitimate businessman. I planned to call my future antique store *The Little Oak*.

About six weeks after I left my old life, I was reading the *Dallas Morning News* as I usually did with breakfast when a small piece caught my attention. "Mr. Cleo Washington, an alleged drug dealer and Dallas Club owner, was found dead in his home from what appeared to be a drug overdose." I knew Cleo had a weakness for coke but did not know if he was interested in heroin too. Maybe Vinny had someone "take care" of Mr. Washington and our problem. I had mixed feelings about the news. I was very happy the immediate problem was over with, but it left the question was Vinny behind this? This was not my first face with unpleasant reality, Mexican jail was no kindergarten, but that was more physical un-pleasant with minimum mental torture. This would be a question unanswered, did the end justify the means? The whole thing left me uncomfortable, especially since it took me a few days to reach Vinny, but when I did, he confirmed, Without Cleo's testimony the law has no case or evidence so now our problem is over." At least for now, but I knew that I was on someone's radar and probably my name was on "the list" of potential drug dealers in the area. I would have to be much more attentive to details.

I had applied to Southern Methodist University in Dallas to work on a Master of Business Administration degree and had already been accepted before my summer problem began. At least I was free of worrying about two government entities, the U.S. Army and the local draft board. Rodger and I rented a two-bedroom apartment for the summer in Dallas and moved out of Denton.

At the same time, I also rented a small eight-hundred square-foot store front on Greenville Avenue in a very eclectic East Dallas neighborhood, a great location for the antique store I wanted to open. I ordered a set of awnings printed with "The Little Oak" to shade the two windows out front. I covered the interior walls in vertical, fresh-cut cedar one-by-twelve boards to give the inside a rustic look. I started attending auctions of European furniture pieces imported from overseas by wholesalers. To fill the store, I also added some of my own furniture from my old Denton house that I did not have room for in the apartment. I planned to open the store in five or six weeks, after the completion of my fall business. With my mom's help the store would be manned while I was at school, leaving my pot deliveries for the weekends.

I called Colonel Gutrez to work out the details of this year's transactions, but I could sense something was wrong when he did not give me much of a battle over the new price. He said he was ready for me to make the first pick-up the following week. I sensed something was not kosher, but I did not want to miss a whole year of business, so I ignored my vague misgivings and bad feelings.

Rule Number Nine: Experience is merely the name we give our mistakes.

Just the same, I made this first run of the season without David McCullum. Rodger met me at the Del Rio ranch sites, where I picked up the cash and left the plane's seats with him and flew off to complete the first dance of the year, money for pot. This time when I reached our designated highway, I did a fly-by and when I did not find anything out of order I started to land, the front tires had just touched on the ground when I began hearing gunshots exploding and saw illuminating projectiles race by the cockpit to my left. I could see muzzle fire off in the distance. I did not wait to find out who, what, and why as I was already heading back north.

As I headed back to the border in Texas my gut told me someone was watching me. I dropped my altitude, decreased my speed and cut the lights. Sure enough, in just minutes another plane passed overhead, thank you, David McCullum for his lesson about how to be stealthy when necessary.

When I got back to the drop site to meet Rodger, I found no lights from the truck; in fact, no truck, no Rodger. I had only one choice, fly back to the airport in San Antonio without the seats. This would cost me. The shit was about to hit the fan.

I called my attorney and asked him to locate Rodger in a jail somewhere. Hours later Abe informed me that Rodger was being held in the Brackettville County jail, having been arrested for trespassing. The truck had $3,000 cash in the glove box and, of course, those damn seats from the airplane. Thankfully, Rodger followed the one and only rule when arrested, keep your mouth shut. Abe got him out on $2,000 bail the next morning. Inexplicably, the rancher never pressed charges. This fiasco cost me on multiple levels. Attorney bill, bail bond, and the $500 cash deposit on the plane because I returned it missing the seats. Amazingly, the $3,000 cash in the glovebox seemed to have disappeared; it had not been logged into evidence with the plane's seats. When all was over, I still had to get the seats in Brackettville picked up and delivered back to the San Antonio airport where I had rented the plane in the first place.

Things could have been much worse if I had been busted again in Mexico or in Texas. Those shots were meant as a warning and I really owed Gutrez, or someone, a big thanks. I figured it was not in the Colonel's best interest for me to be busted and then involve him, so he must have arranged the timely shots. Our government was still putting lots of pressure on Mexico to curb the flow of drugs into the states. Though we had a good thing going for a while, I never spoke to him again. I called his number once some time had passed, but it belonged to someone else.

Both Rodger and I were lucky to get out of this mess with so little wear and tare.

The season of 1971 was pretty much over for me. I did a few 50 to 300-pound deals with a much smaller profit line. I had my clothing market customers, though I really missed the profits and the excitement from the bigger deals.

I did not sit around feeling sorry for myself. Instead, I put my energy into the new antique store. I flew to England over the Christmas holidays where I bought three shipping containers of European furnishings, including some glassware, though I knew nothing about it at the time, the pretty sales lady convinced me the glassware would sell very well. **"The door of success is marked 'push' and 'pull'. "Achieving success is knowing when to do what."** Besides whom am I to argue with a pretty lady?

The Little Oak opened quietly. The containers from Europe arrived just in time. I had paid about $4,000 to $5,000 each for the antiques but would end up making $20,000 to $25,000 in retail sales from each of the shipping containers.

Rodger moved back to Denton. I rented a small Cape Cod style home not far from the store in East Dallas and SMU. My mom was enlisted to work in the store, so I could go to class. She added a woman's touch by bringing in several potted plants to place on the tables to brighten the atmosphere. If left to most guys, we would still be living in caves and only once in a while would we drag our animal skins out and shake them off to air them out.

Surprisingly, the plants became a great add-on sale item for the store after many customers came in to buy a lamp or an end table but ended up adding a plant. Eventually, we established a clientele who came for just the plants. We started to carry many varieties of ferns, dieffenbachia, corn plants, philodendrons, and miniature trees. The citrus trees made the store smell wonderful when they flowered, which prompted me to add herbs and spices to the aroma in the store. As a customer walked through the store and brushed against a ginger plant or sage bush, they would inadvertently diffuse a new fragrance throughout the showroom.

My spare time is non-existent now. One day and two nights a week I was in classes. Most Saturday nights and Sundays, I found myself trucking to Austin or Houston to pick up pot from Rudy or Dan and then deliver it afterwards. I could make the short runs to Oklahoma or Arkansas at night after classes or when the store was closed. I did not get a lot of sleep. It was the long runs to South Louisiana or to Arizona that I had to be creative. I found a wholesale cactus dealer just outside Tucson, so I brought Marijuana to Evan and returned with freshly dug Arizona Cactus win win. The season for the wholesale side of the pot sales was in only a few months so somehow it worked.

I finally had to hire another person to help me in the store on a full-time basis, someone to take care of the day-to-day management of the furniture business, which would free me up to concentrate on my more profitable green sales. Frances Vogel walked in one morning to look for a Queen Anne Chair. Even though we did not have it we talked for almost two hours about plants, art, and politics. Frances was very knowledgeable about design and style. After he told me he was between jobs, I hired him before he left with his house plants. I believed he would help bring in a more affluent clientele looking for real antiques, not just nice old furniture. Most importantly, I felt I could trust him.

By the end of July 1972, I got that old itchy feeling, like a kid who knows Christmas is coming. The adrenalin rushes every time I think about it. The fall harvest was just around the corner, and I had another idea that I had been developing. I had once asked Rudy what area of

Mexico most of his grass came from, and he divulged a couple of the main areas. Why not just go down there myself and hunt for my next source and buy right out of the fields like I did in Oklahoma? I had enough working capital to buy directly from anyone. If I could work out the logistics, I could be back in the wholesale business.

I left for Mexico by myself in my Ford truck in the first week of August 1972. After a day of scouting the area Juan had spoken of and asking questions, I got the answer I was looking for, but not what I wanted to hear. Most of those growers had contracts for their products before they were ever planted.

I was at my wit's end at the end of the second day. So much beautiful marijuana and I could not find the right person to sell it to me. While filling up the truck at a small petrol station just out of town, I struck up a conversation with a fieldworker who was refueling his employer's truck at the pump next to mine. Eventually, I casually inquired about any "special" crops in the area that could be bought?

"My boss, he knows everyone around here. He probably will know." I followed him back to the field where he was working and let him approach his boss to fill him in on the situation. I met Jorge Lopez and his son-in-law Alejandro, Señor Lopez was over six and half feet tall and weighed over 300 pounds though he seemed to glide gracefully over the freshly cultivated ground as he approached me. I studied his face which was tanned leather from many hours in the sun. He stuck out his well-worn, callous hand. "Jorge Lopez," he said, "this is my small farm. What can I do for you, Señor?" His eyes seemed to drill into my core.

I extended my hand, "Max Gold, Señor, you have such a beautiful place here, I am envious." We spoke of the weather and family and such before we got down to real business. It was suppertime, so he invited me to eat with him and his men in the field. We sat around a small wood fire, warming our tortillas, beans, and chilies. We did not speak much during dinner, but after Jorge brought out a bottle of tequila with which we toasted each other and each other's Presidents and a couple other people that I do not remember. I'm sure Jorge wanted me thick-headed before negotiations started to see what I was made of.

"Max, I was born right there, in that old shack. My family was very poor, and I have had to work in these fields since I was a small child, growing beans and peppers. So how did you get into the marijuana business?" I gave him a short version, telling of my purchasing experiences from a government official but did not mention any names. Jorge only shook his head in an understanding way. "That is the way it is. We peasants do all the work and the powers-that-be make all the money."

I knew that the yields of most fields were being purchased for $28 to $30 a pound. He had only 5,000 kilos or 11,000 pounds left. We settled for $40 a pound for the straight product, no special packaging, and we set up the delivery for the second week of September. When all was said and done, I was buying the product for less than ever before and knew that the next year's purchase was already made. I too now had a contract for 20,000 pounds of next year's crop. I would own next year's whole field at a better price than today's purchase. I was back in business and feeling an amazing adrenaline rush of excitement. Making a deal is as addictive as any poppy drug.

Jorge asked, "Max, would you like to come home with me to spend the night?"

"Thank you, Señor, but I think if it's okay with you, I would like to sleep out here under the sky with the guys. It's just too peaceful out here."

This seemed to strike a chord in him. "I remember as a boy doing just that many a night, but now I am too old to sleep on the ground. My back can't take it anymore. Amigo, we will be doing lots of business from now on, I think, Bueno Noches." When we shook hands, I again noticed I was holding a laborer's hands.

I arranged for my flight instructor, David McCullum and a few of his friends to make several trips each for which they rented Aero Commander 500, twin-engine planes that could haul about 1,500 pounds a trip. Jorge had assembled plenty of help. This was not the first time these workers had done this, so they formed a line and did not take very long to load the bundles. I paid the fly guys $10,000 a trip. They covered their own expenses for planes and fuel. We made these trips over two different weekends in September, using our old friends Jim's grass runway just outside Del Rio. The first trip was uneventful. The last trip though the crew ran into a really bad storm, I missed it because I had come down a couple days earlier to supervise weighing and packaging. It enabled me to see the whole process from planting to smoking. I contacted most of my old client base. I had lost a few buyers and dropped a couple others myself, but two of my best customers and friends turned me on to a volume buyer in Arkansas. For referrals, I always added bonus packages of primo stashes, or gave them tighter prices on what they bought. Most of my regulars were glad I was back with fresh product. I had always taken care of any problems they had with the grass they purchased from me, like too many stems in the bricks or a mistake in the weight of a brick.

I moved all 11,276 pounds in less than six weeks. Rodger was as glad to get back into the game as I was. I had not seen a lot of him since the bust. He seemed to be going through some thing and had gone into hiding, probably with that new bimbo from New York who I met briefly, and who seemed to be dominating his time.

1973

Pink Floyd released the amazing "Dark Side of the Moon "album and the Rolling Stones' have the number one single, the classic "Angie".

OPEC nations agree among themselves to cut back oil production, gas prices are up 200% a gallon almost overnight.

Vice President Spiro Agnew is force to resign after he was charged by IRS, for Tax Evasion, and taking bribes.

In January 1973 the Military Draft ended.

The biggest issue of 1973 was Abortion, the United States Supreme Court finally got **Roe verses Wade** in front of them and the outcome was abortion rights for all women and it denies any government the right, to tell a woman what they can and cannot do to their own bodies.

Paul McCarthy is arrested for growing marijuana on his farm in England.

I dated several women over the years, both Jewish and non-Jewish woman. Some were a few years older and some younger. There was no shortage of attractive women in Dallas I also found that many lonely, bored wives would come in the store and would flirt with me. I had more than a few propositions. The biggest truth was, I never really totally got over Debbie. We could talk for hours or just hang out and not say a word even though we knew what each other was thinking or needing. We had been comfortable with each other, and I missed that a lot. It was more than just sex; it was the intimacy we shared. So, I guess I was comparing each of these women to her. I also had some anger issues over the way she split and then never a word again. I did get one small cut out of a newspaper article about a small-town bank robbery gone badly, guard being shot, and in critical condition, in an unmarked envelope from Alpine Texas. No date and no name or even a small hello, so I can only guess? I even broke down and called her mom. She just hung up on me when she found out who it was.

Now the military draft had finally ended I was free from that green threat. I was busy with school, and although I did not have my heart in it, I was still pursuing my MBA. The Little Oak's business seemed to grow steadily, and I was amazed by how many plants we were selling. We took deliveries of new plants at least twice a week. This brought in a constant flow of new customers. At the end of January 1973, I decided to look for a building where I could expand the business and add a greenhouse as well to grow my own legal plants. The building I found and eventually bought was just down the street from my original store. It had 4,500 square feet of showroom, plus it had a couple of offices and, most importantly, there was a large parking lot in front and on one side. The side parking area is where the new green house was going to go. It took me nine months to get a variance from the city to build the project. I had to go in front of the city council and had to deal with zoning boards. I had to fight with neighborhood groups. I am amazed by how any progress is made in a city based on what I had to go through.

I finally got my permits and had a 15-foot by 35-foot glass greenhouse built with modern conveniences. The roofs could be opened during the summer to let out built-up heat and it had two gas heaters for winter. I hired one full-time grower to do all the propagation and sprout new plants. I also hired two high school girls to work part-time in the green house or the store as needed.

Although the whole renovation process was a royal pain in the ass, in the long run it turned out to be a good decision. I provided my bank with a year's worth of business financials and had a good down payment. I was able to get a loan sizable enough to purchase the building, add the new greenhouse and to make all the needed improvements to the property, including some roof repairs, bathroom renovations and a general spiffing up.

1974

President Ford also gives amnesty to some military deserters from the Vietnam.

Gas is fifty- five cents a gallon.

New cars averaged $3750.

President Gerald Ford gives President Nixon a complete pardon for his federal crimes.

Mohamad Ali who lost his crown and ability to fight in 1967 has his first big shot back in the ring. The Rumble in the Jungle, found him against a, twenty- five year old undefeated champion, called George Foreman The match was set in Kinshasa Zaire, whose people love Ali, and they would chant as he worked out. Ali won with an eighth- round knockout.

The new speed limit on the highways was 55 MPH.

The new store, "The Oak", opened in the early part of January,74. One of my mom's old friends, Helen Blotnic, who was a widow, came to work at the new store. She had been an interior decorator in New York when my mom first knew her. This was an easy transition for her. She first came thinking of working only part-time, but she was a walking book of knowledge. Helen had impeccable taste and Francis followed her around like a puppy dog, absorbing anything she would share. Although my overhead was rising at the new store, so were my profit margins.

I had kept the smaller location for storage but also a place to sell the low-end furnishings, now that I was acquiring more expensive items for the new store. The old store, or the "Little Nut" as she was now called, was still getting the hippie or younger crowds, people who were looking for bargains and buyers on a strict budget. It also was another outlet for my house plants.

One thing did happen at the same time that almost sealed the closing of the Little Nut. At about 10:00 in the morning I had just finished making my bi-weekly deposit at the bank when a long-haired fellow came into the store. There was something off about him; my adrenalin started churning and my heartbeat quickened. My sixth sense again. I slowly approached him with all my senses heightened. "Is MM around?" he asked. He was nervous and constantly scanning the room.

I replied, "No one here with that name, but if you need any furnishings or house plants, I am glad to help. "

He was smiling when he replied, "Yeah, man, I need some plants to smoke and I have cash, lots and I heard I could get hooked up here."

"You have heard wrong. If that is all you are interested in, you need to look elsewhere." He was stubborn, so it took me a few minutes and a threat to call the police to get rid of him.

What worried me was that none of my marijuana buyers knew anything about my antique stores. It was a cardinal rule never to do business at home or, in this case, my workplace. I would find out later that day that he had been to the new store as well; looking for MM. Francis had run him off but started asking questions. I cooled his interest with a bullshit story of a friend of mine and how a while back I was inadvertently present when he did a deal. "Francis, if anyone comes in and asks for pot again, just call the police and take down their license tag numbers," I told him in the most earnest of terms. That seemed to satisfy him.

This was not the end of getting calls or a visit or two at The Little Oak from people looking for MM. One guy actually asked for the Marijuana Man. There were different voices on the phone claiming to be someone I knew from the old days or a dealer that I knew been busted in the past? I answered each one the same way. I could not help them except to sell furniture or houseplants. That was all. If they called back, I would bring in the authorities. I never asked why they had called or who gave them my name. I did not want to show too much interest. I did believe Special Agent Longstead was trying an old fishing technique, but he could not get me to bite.

I had made a commitment to my mom to attend the wedding of one of my cousins with her and my dad in June. Even though I was not close to my cousin or her mom, my aunt, I was getting the Jewish mother's guilt trip to convince me. When she called to remind me, "Oh mom I thought the date was for next year you know June 75," I replied. She was not going for it so under protest I agreed to go.

Now at the wedding, one of my cousin's bridesmaids immediately stuck out as she was more beautiful than the bride. She was a classic Jewish beauty with dark, curly hair. Her eyes were very bright, almost glittering, and though her mouth was not large, her lips seemed like they were whispering to me. The most impressive feature was her smile; it lit up the space around her. The rest of her body was tight at 5'6" and at most 115 pounds, I guessed.

I had heard the phrase, "Love at first "sight," but thought it was just a writer's expression. But my stomach was doing the wav and I could feel my breathing change. All I could do was keep staring. I did not know what was happening to me. I have never been so strongly drawn to anyone like this before, not even Debbie. Hell, I had not even heard her voice or talked to her and I knew nothing about her, but I was struck. I remember my Mom looking at me during the ceremony. I must have had a strange expression or something because she whispered in my ear, "Are you all right?" I don't remember much of the marital ceremony or the vows and only vaguely remember the breaking of the glass by the groom. At the reception I was actually nervous to go up to her and introduce myself. I am not normally the shy type, but my hands were sweating, and it seemed important for me to make a good first impression.

As I sat at our assigned table, I found myself exchanging glances and a few smiles with her. I was picking at my chicken and just about to make my move when I looked up to see her standing in front of me. She spoke first, "Hello Maximillian. My name is Tina Chavanoff. Are you going to ask me to dance?"

"The greatest of pleasure to do so, I assure you, Miss Tina," I replied as I stood up and looked into the most unusual eyes, with two-toned irises. Around her dark pupils were gold rings adjoining another ring of light brown.

Tina was from Tulsa. "Paula told me she had a cute single cousin who would be here tonight, and since those two older gentlemen in the corner are the only other single guys here, I figure you must be Max."

"No, actually my name is Ringo, that kid dancing with his little sister is Max, I think." We both laughed and danced for most of the night. I learned she was working part-time as a massage therapist and attending the University of Tulsa to get her Master's in art history. She did most of the talking; I just added a few comments here and there. I told her a little bit about myself, though not about my pot business. I told her about my antique stores and how I, too, was getting my Masters. We ate a little, danced a little, and laughed a lot. I took her out to the parking lot to get some air. "Do you want to burn one?" I asked?

As I pulled out a joint, Tina giggled, "Sure. I thought you might smoke some." It was one of the most enchanting nights of my life

We said our good nights to our family and friends. The bride and groom had already left, and I followed Tina back to her room in the hotel where we talked until almost three a.m. though she was leaving in the morning, and we both needed some sleep. I finally related what I was feeling, "Tina, I want to spend a lot more time with you."

Tina replied, "I feel the same way." She confessed that her reaction at first seeing me was similar to mine when I first glimpsed her. "That's why I had to come over to you."

We agreed I would fly to Tulsa the next Friday night to spend the weekend with her. We kissed several times before I left.

Her last question before I left was, "Maxie, where do you get such good smoke?"

I just knew this was going to be something very special, especially if she could get her head around my marijuana business. The next five days were like the time I had back in the Mexican jail, verrrry looong. Tina and I talked by phone daily, the high point of my twenty- four hours.

When Tina picked me up at the airport, we stopped at a small Chinese restaurant called Supreme Love for dinner then back to her place. I fired up a twisted bird while she cranked up the stereo. We must have both been in heat because soon we were in her bedroom where we were to spend Friday night and a lot of Saturday. I had never been so horny or so satisfied. I tried everything I knew or read about with her and her with me. By Saturday night we were sexually exhausted, the best type of fatigue. We showered together, got dressed, ate at an Italian eatery. Tina had crab-stuffed Ravioli, and I had a peppercorn steak accompanied by spaghetti with spicy tomato gravy. If I had died right then and there, I would have gone to heaven contented. After dinner we went to a club to listen to some great jazz. By the time we got back to Tina's we were worn out and slept like the dead. I awoke the next morning to the smell of bacon and eggs. We drank tea as neither of us liked coffee.

"Tell me, where do you score such great weed?" Tina seductively asked for the second time in a week.

I turned toward her and smiled, "I've got some pretty good connections."

I told her before I left that evening, "I have never felt this way about anyone before and want you to move in with me. I know this is fast, and we have only known each other for a week, but it just feels right."

"I will come back to Dallas next weekend, and we'll talk about it then," Tina replied, before we kissed.

As soon as my plane left the ground for home, I felt I was missing a part of myself. The next week went painfully slow again even though we talked every night. It was a poor substitute for being in her sun-shinny presence.

At the beginning of July in 1974, I had to make a trip to Mexico to visit my fields. I also needed to go to Europe to look for inventory for the furniture stores. I found if I did not go myself and left it up to a supplier, I would end up with a lot of pieces that were odd and ends like a dining room table with only two matching chairs and no cadenza or a China cabinet with drawers or shelves missing. From the containers I also would accumulate a lot of broken pieces that were not quality in the first place or old pieces that were missing important parts like the legs or parts of carved decoration. Some furniture pieces had been carved up to make totally different furniture. I would need someone who could reproduce the needed parts and restore them to their original beauty. I looked into getting some of the items fixed by local talent, mostly with poor results. Often the cost was so high I could never break even, let alone make a profit. I also had had problems in the past opening one of the twenty-foot metal shipping containers only to find that merchandise of lesser quality had been substituted. On a previous trip to England, I had found a beautiful, eighteenth century French provincial writing desk which I had paid top dollar for but got a 1938 knock-off instead. The merchant said the original had already been sold without his knowledge, sorry.

On my return trip to England the next December I went back to the very warehouse where I had been screwed. In his showroom I found my desk, right where I had left it the previous year. I confronted the owner in the middle of his store. The discussion became heated. When I got louder, he vehemently directed me into his office. He challenged me to take him to court with a smug smile. I have never been so mad, but I took my aviators off, looked him dead in the eyes and calmly said," I have a better idea; I'll just do what we do back home in Texas. I'll put a bullet in your fuckin' head and then deal with your business partner or your grieving family over this matter." I unconsciously put my hand into my coat pocket.

He froze and his eyes opened wide. "Okay, Okay, we can work something out. No need to get uncivilized about this misunderstanding."

I bought enough inventories to fill a container at much better prices than in the past. I watched while my prized writing desk and its twin, which I had discovered in the back of his warehouse under a blanket, were crated and loaded on a truck. Word must have spread to the vendors down the street because whenever the strange straw hat and aviator–sunglass-wearing "Texan" came to buy, it always seemed to evoke royal treatment.

I sometimes knowingly paid too much for a piece because I wanted a dealer to put aside merchandise for me when they got their hands on something special. Everyone needs to make a profit, so the buying is as important as the selling. If something is highly coveted, the selling is easy as the price is less important to a discerning client for whom money is not an issue.

I decided I really did not want to be away from the stores for the Mexican and European trips. So I sent Frances and Helen on the buying trip to Europe. It would be a bonus for their great work. Helen wanted to look for special pieces that she knew would be in demand. I sent lots of cash and I was able to wash a little more of my pot profit this way.

Their trip took 14 days and included visiting the Netherlands, northern Italy, and Switzerland, and a cruise through the French countryside. It was in northern Italy that Helen had some of her greatest success. Frances later told me, "She seems to have second sight and great instincts about where to look and what to buy. She bought at dirt low prices things I would have passed on, but now I know, and we'll make a killing on them. I have learned so much and have honed my negotiating skills dealing with some of the shrewdest traders around. We did some sightseeing, but even then we kept our eyes open. Right out of a local's home, Helen bought a French country dining room set. The people were eating on it when we passed by their window. She asked if they were interested in selling the table and chairs. They said, "Oui, " and once we were invited in, she negotiated for a sideboard, copper pots and pans and some old French iron pieces that a true artisan blacksmith must have made over 200 years ago."

One of the things I had also told them before they left was to keep an eye out for unusual plants and to buy seeds. The live plants would not get through customs, but the seeds might not be noticed. They found a few unusual items and even bought some vegetable seeds that we could sprout and offer as something new to the Oak's customers.

Friday finally came and after picking up Tina from the airport, I took her to my new store first. I was proud of what I had accomplished in such a short time. She was impressed with the greenhouse, how well the plants were growing, and the large variety of plants in my inventory. I discovered she loved working in the dirt, organic soil or compost like the girls. "My mom and I use to work together on the flower beds. We would order seed and plant catalogs. From there we would design each year's looks with colors and textures." Tina asked the girls working in this tropical environment a lot of questions. She seemed to have a lot more knowledge of growing, grafting, and sprouting than I ever had. I was learning more about her every day. The more I found, the more I liked and the more I liked, the more I became enamored. I was hooked and would probably have asked her to marry me right then to avoid losing her. It was not a thought I shared with anyone else, though.

After lunch we went by the Little Nut where she fell in love with the space and the neighborhood with its collection of specialty stores selling vintage shoes and clothing, the art galleries, Old World bakers, tailor shop, wine bar, French restaurant, as well as Ethiopian, Italian, and Middle Eastern restaurants. The area was a mix of different cultures and people, young and old. There was an Irish pub next to a Chinese hole-in-the-wall and a jewelry store that specialized in estate sale pieces and old silver. My favorite was an old hamburger joint with '50s décor and an old jukebox full of classic rock-and-roll. This was the neighborhood that had drawn me to the area in the first place.

The homes behind these businesses were built in the '20s and '30s, all-brick homes with fine detail in the outside and inside construction. Some were traditional, others were in the Cape Cod, or Swiss Chalet styles. Many had beautiful stained-glass windows while others had my favorite: cut- beveled glass windows. Some were small one-story homes; others were large, two to two and a half stories on large estate lots with their own mature trees and landscaping, each unique but charming.

I had to run a few errands, one to the bank and one to the upholstery shop which was redoing an old Victorian couch. "Do you want to come?"

"No, I'm going to explore the shops in the area and get a feel for things in the neighborhood." I was beginning to think I might be able to convince Tina to move in with me.

When I came back, Stacy, my part-timer was helping a customer, and Tina was selling a young couple an old oak queen bed, dressers and end tables. She also convinced them they needed a full-length floor mirror by titillating them with what they could see if they were to place the mirror beside their new bed. Tina expanded the sale by adding several ferns and a couple of corn plants. She was a natural salesperson. I was pleasantly surprised, and she was ecstatic.

When I showed my place to Tina, I had an exuberance of the moment and I felt like picking her up in my arms and carrying her across the threshold, but with a second consideration, thought better of it. We came through the small galley kitchen past the dining room table where I suavely laid my hat, the leather pouch along with my sunglasses. From there to the living room on to the bedrooms and that only took just a blink of an eye. Once in the master suit, I turned to her and quickly said, "This could be your bedroom, too."

Tina just smiled. "We'll see," was her reply as she began undressing. If this was going to be a repeat of the previous weekend, I was eager, naked and, like a hungry bee, all over that sweet flower. I was in love and falling deeper every second of the time I spent with Tina. We spent a lot of time smoking weed and just talking, cuddling, laughing and sharing simple things like feeding each other grapes, which of course led to the Great Grape Fight of June 1974.

Later, after we showered and dressed for dinner, I took Tina out to the covered front porch. As we sat on the old metal swing, I began a discussion that I was not looking forward to. "I need to discuss something important with you." I began to explain about my marijuana business. I wanted her to be fully aware of the illegal side of my lifestyle while still trying to stress the importance it played in my life. If she and I were going to be a part of each other's lives, I needed to be honest and tell her the complications of my life. I explained my wholesale operation, again leaving out specifics, no names or locations. The less she knew the better for her.

She was fascinated and quite surprised. Tina had lots of questions, like "Do your folks know? Do the employees of the stores know?" I answered each question one at a time while explaining I was buying large quantities from a farmer in Mexico and then selling it in smaller quantities to other dealers. My exposure was less that way. I was simply a trader. I explained my business rules and how they limited my exposure, but that I had been busted in Mexico years earlier and that I was on the government's radar as a potential dealer. I told Tina a little bit about Debbi and the story about what she had gone through in Mexico and then in Denton how she became radicalized and left. "Look T, I do not mix my pot business and the stores." Though actually, not totally true, but close enough. "So, if worst came to worst they cannot take the businesses from me and I do have a legal source of income."

Tina's last remark before we left for dinner was, "If it is so dangerous, why not quit and let it rest?" A good, no, great question, that I had asked myself more than once every day. I think that, the money aside, it is the adrenaline of the whole process. Mexico, the drive with illegal product, the people like me who I deal with, all this makes for an addiction that I had come to need to make my life real and exciting.

"As long as I follow the rules, I'll be safe." I proudly exclaimed.

We went to an Ethiopian restaurant where customers eat with their hands, and we finished the conversation over the next few hours. "Tina, I have been doing this since 1966, and I really love what I do. I'm providing an exceptional product too many people that are hungry for, the Brotherhood of the Smoke's magic. Aren't you hungering for some right now?" I chuckled. "I take very good care of my business and will never involve you directly and will never intentionally put you in any danger. But I want you to take this information seriously before you make any decision."

Tina stayed the whole two weeks while the employee group was in Europe, spending some of her day working at the Little Nut. She loved rearranging the inventory to her own taste and made up stories about the people who originally owned the piece way back when. That first Sunday morning we went to the east Texas town Canton. We look for bargains. I bought a couple of items for which I paid cash. Yes, it helps in the negotiations. If there is a price tag of $1,500, I say, "Here is $1,150 cash." The seller is going to contemplate having cash now or maybe more money later. How much later? He'll think about having to reload it back on the truck. Cash wins most of the time. I bought a lovely mahogany-framed beveled glassed make-up mirror for Tina as a gift for all her hard work. I tried to pay her for the time she lost as a massage therapist, but she turned my cash down. I even suggested that I could build her a small studio in the back of the Little Nut if she wanted to continue her massage therapy work.

One day I was busy all day running errands and meeting with the store's accountant. When I finally got back to the store, I did my best Ricky Ricardo, "Lucy, I'm home," routine. This got me a hard- deep laugh from my girl. I kissed the tears of joy from her eyes. After locking the front doors, we ended up naked in the back office. That old squeaking office chair had never had such a workout as when we were rolling around in passion and excitement. It was hard to control Tina and the chair; we ended up falling out and landing on the floor. No worse for wear, but it did not end our passion. We were still kids with a new toy.

Thursday afternoon Tina left early to shop and go home to cook us a homemade meal of lobster, asparagus, stuffed baked potatoes, light salad, Moscato wine, and a Key lime pie. This was a pattern I could easily get used to and I don't know if I could have been any happier.

After I had praised her for such a great meal, she spoke to me in such a loving voice. "Max you are really a mess, but I think I fell in love way back when Paula first spoke about you to me, long before we even met."

My reply was simple, "I love you too and if you want to keep this a weekend and holiday relationship until we work everything out, if that is what you think that is best for you. I'll take whatever time you have for me."

The ten o'clock news that night concerned the latest on Watergate and its newest information about President Nixon. "It looks like Nixon may be the first President since Andrew Johnson to be impeached. I guess Tricky Dick was not that tricky." I'd yelled to bathroom as Tina was getting ready for bed.

"The man is a disgrace," she replied, "I always thought he was so creepy looking, how his wife could make love to him? Buuuurrr, no way."

I still had to make my trip to Mexico when the travelers came back from Europe. Also, I still wanted to find a better way to deal with the biggest problem of the business, getting the product over the border safely and reliably.

Tina wanted to give us a try. So, we flew to Tulsa Friday night and began packing her belongings. Saturday morning, I rented a U-Haul 14' box truck, and we worked all day Saturday and a good part of Sunday to get her belongings all loaded.

As we were packing Saturday morning, we discussed some basic topics that we both felt need to be addressed and made some basic agreements to help avoid, as much as possible, any day-to-day discord. She told me what she expected from me now and in the future, and I likewise expressed my expectations. We both felt it was better to get these issues addressed right then rather than when she is chewing me out over a left up toilet seat, but really being pissed off over something totally different. My folks had been married over forty years, and they had a good marriage but sometimes fought. We even discussed fair fighting guidelines because we knew we would have some disagreements.

"The only thing I really ask of you Max is honesty, and for us not to go to bed mad, but to work things out before we sleep. I really can't stand unresolved issues."

I had told her before that I would not involve her in any of my grass business at all and she would have to trust me that I knew what I was doing. Sometimes she might not know where I was or where I was going but that I would always keep in touch. I explained that we would not be getting any pot business calls at the house or stores, and that I would not be keeping much product at the house. I also reassured her I would not deal with anything but marijuana. She would probably never meet any of the people I was doing business with or their families.

"Tina, since you are going to be my mate forever, so what do you think about children?" I smiled.

"Well Maxie you know I grew up as a single child, the only living relative I have left is in Atlanta. She was my father's older sister and I hardly see or talk to her." Her parents had both been killed by a drunk driver during her sophomore year of college. I was her first non-girl roommate, and we were going to be starting a relationship that she greatly wanted, and we both greatly needed. Tina was not a needy, clingy type of person, rather just the opposite. She gave of herself unconditionally. I saw it every day we worked together and as she interacted with customers and fellow employees. I loved her for her ability to give so much of herself. "How about we start with two and go from there?" she finally concluded.

I was brought up in a large family with lots of relatives and was very independent, probably a bit self-centered and spoiled I admit. In the future, I needed to be more aware of her needs and less on my own, which was going to be hard. "I was thinking a dozen and go from there, "I laughed.

"Okay, we agree," she giggled, "somewhere between two and twelve." By the end of that Saturday night, we both had a good understanding of each other's needs and expectations. She had a small trust left by her folks. That helped her through college and paid for some of the expenses that her massage business didn't cover.

I had promised to build a little private studio in the back of the Little Nut for her massage business and for her to have a little space of her own. She thought that she might transfer to SMU to finish up her master's, and I knew I had at least one person I could count on to show up and work at the Little Nut.

I drove the truck while Tina followed in her little orange VW Bug convertible. We arrived back in Dallas early Monday morning. We were tired and operated on not much sleep but truly happy.

When the group of travelers got back from Europe, I held a debriefing at our house. After the tea and crumpets that Tina served, we all looked over the Polaroid pictures they had taken of the purchases and made a list of incoming items, approximate cost, what the item might sell for and which store to send it to. "I want you all to go through your list of clients and decorators and let them know what is coming in soon." The pot business had taught me that the faster the item moves from your ownership to the new owner, the sooner you get paid. That's what business is essentially all about.

Frances took me aside later and thanked me profusely. "I learned so much about the buying process and negotiation side of the business. Thank you again so much." Helen also came to me before she left to call my mother, I'm sure, to thank me and to drop off a little thank you gift. An unusual silver cufflink set. "It has been one of the most enjoyable times of my life, and I glad you trusted me enough to make the choices that we made," she said.

I took the vegetable and flower seeds that Frances had brought back into the greenhouse the first thing the next morning. I had the crew start spouting the new varieties to see what colors and textures were going to grow. My folks had met Tina at my cousin's wedding, of course, but they did not realize we had developed such a deep relationship so fast and that we were now living together. It did not take long for my mom to get wind when Helen came back from the trip. Mom was very happy for us and called Tina to invite us over for Sabbat Friday night dinner. I am sure Mom would have rather it have happened after a wedding, but times were different, and she understood. My ladies did not take long to bond. The chemistry between them was amazing. Tina really missed her mom and my mom had missed a mother- daughter connection since after my sister Judy married and moved out of the area. They quickly scheduled a spa date for the next week. I guess it was a different kind of bonding ritual with women; I could not imagine myself going to get a massage and shvitz with Harold.

Now that everybody was back to work and Tina was set up, I left for Mexico. When I got to the fields there, I was surprised at how large and tall the plants had gotten. Overall, the Oklahoma marijuana plants were bushier and much shorter. These plants in front of me could pass for tall Christmas trees. Alejandra told me it would be a few weeks before they would be ready to harvest and would take a few more weeks to dry and package, so it looked like the end of August or first of September as usual. He also indicated that the field I was looking at would bring over 11,000 kilos, over 24,000 pounds. "Senor, are you going to be able to come up with that much cash?" As more people got into the marijuana business it became more competitive than when I had first started, so if I could not come up with the cash, someone else certainly would. Over lunch I asked Alejandro, "Do you know of any truckers who I might contact to haul my purchase over the U.S. border?"

"I don't know of any, but Jorge knows everyone and I will call him to see what he suggests."

Later that afternoon Jorge came by and greeted me with a big bear hug like I was a long- lost son. He had put on even more weight since the last time I had seen him. "Max, I just got married to a younger woman who wanted many children, so I am trying to watch my weight and keep her busy." He winked and laughed.

"Jorge, I too have a new wonderful lady," I happily informed him. As in prior visits, we all sat around the fire, eating, drinking cold Mexican beer and talking "I am not ready for kids yet," I mumbled.

"Hell," Jorge said, "if you wait until you are ready, you will never be ready for children. Mi amigo, Ninos are what brings you real joy and meaning in life." After the field hands left and there were just the three of us, he broke out a large joint and we got very stoned.

In a break in the conversation I asked, "Jorge, do you have any contacts with American truckers who I might get to make a few trips hauling my stuff?

Jorge smiled, "I tell you a story first. This story starts with Uncle Paco, my mother's brother. He had been in the smuggling business up and down the American-Mexican border for many years, beginning back in the 1920s when he was trading in liquor. I had grown up helping him smuggle people, tropical birds, and some pot when we were living near Del Rio. Things were easy then. You paid someone to look away and everyone was happy. Now you could still pay someone to look away, but that does not actually guarantee you very much. I'll make a few inquiries and let you know in the morning. Do you want to come home with me, amigo?"

"Thank you again, but I probably would not get much sleep with you two newlyweds."

With a genuine smile, he said, "Adios."

Alejandro told me his father- in- law's main "small" home alone was over 20,000 square feet. "I would expect nothing less from, Jorge," I replied. I fell asleep listening to one of the field hands playing guitar and singing, just a little off key, a song of love lost and love found. This was the life.

Alejandro came back early in the morning just after the sun rose and got the men moving. He gave me the name of a trucker who worked both sides of the border, trucking legal and illegal goods. He told me of a truck stop outside of Laredo that the trucker, Lee Daniel, uses. "Thank you, Alejandro, and please thank Jorge for me. I'll be in touch in a month or so."

When I got back to the border crossing, it was a slow-moving process, so I got a chance to watch how the U.S. Customs and Border Patrol worked, what they seemed to stop and what they just passed through. It took over an hour for my turn to cross. My mind flashed back to just a few years earlier when I was swimming across the water that was flowing under me now.

When I pulled up to the border guard, he asked, "Where have you been, business or pleasure?" I had done this many times by then, so I was prepared. I had had some business cards made up with my name and bogus phone number and address. The card stated I was a wholesale buyer of fruits and vegetables. After a quick look in my truck, he passed me through, so very easy.

I drove through Laredo and headed up interstate 35 to the truck stop and began making some inquiries. The fuel supervisor knew of my driver. He checked his records and noted none of that driver's trucks had been fueled up there in the last few days. I also checked with one of the older waitresses in the restaurant. Yeah, she also knew my guy but had not seen him lately. "But Hun, if you leave me your business card and a nice tip, I'll make sure he gets it when he shows up." I thanked her and left her a nice tip but no card. Next, I checked the truckers' lounge to ask about my man, but here again I had no luck. I did not like the idea of spending days at a fuel stop waiting for someone who might sometime or other show up. Still mentally considering my next move, I literally bumped into a "lot lizard," a truck stop hooker. After I had apologized profusely for my distracted clumsiness, she asked for a light. She also asked if I had any needs she could help me with.

As I lit her cigarette, I asked about if she had seen my guy.

"No, but have you looked in the Yellow Pages?" Well, from the mouths of... Anyway, I looked in the finger- walking book and found a listing for Lee Daniel's trucking out of McAllen, Texas.

I called and though Lee was not there, he was due back that night. I asked the lady at the end of the phone when it would be the best time to call him in the morning. "About 10:00," she said. "He has to go to town early to get some parts for one of the trucks, but he should be back by then." I had spent two and half hours at that truck stop, although one look in the Yellow Pages would have done the trick. Sometimes the obvious is overlooked.

I got back into my old Ford and headed toward McAllen, just 120 miles away. The news on the radio was full of nothing but the resignation of President Richard Nixon and his successor, Vice President Gerald Ford. Tina and I had talked about this just a few days ago and we made a bet. I lost.

I drove to a small motel outside of McAllen, checked in, and then called Tina to let her know I was okay but had a little bit of work left. She asked if the trip was going well. I told her, "Better than I expected." We talked about the stores a little and I told her I would be home in a few days and to "keep the light on for me," a code phase we had set up to let her know I was really okay. I found a small bar and grille where I ate a large chicken fried steak with the best cream gravy for dinner.

Mc Allen is not a large city but is not a one-street town either. The area is surrounded by lots of small to large fruit and vegetable truck farms and cattle ranches. Also, it had a lot of grapefruit orchards dotted with oil and gas wells. McAllen was the area's service center with lots of farm equipment dealers, car part stores, repair shops and other typical small businesses that are the core of small-town U.S.A. commerce.

After dinner, I got a map of the area and found the way to Lee Daniel's home, which as it turned out, was only ten minutes from my motel, out in the country, which pretty much describes most of the area. I had stopped at Walmart and bought a swimsuit, so when I got back to my room, I changed into my new trunks and took a nice long swim in the pool. I was joined by a couple of kids from San Antonio, in town with their parents to visit relatives. This information was given to me without my asking by the six-year-old boy. His sister was much too shy to talk. At 9: 00 it began to get dark, and I went into my room and got ready for bed.

The next morning, I got up and leisurely got ready for the day. I went back to the grille for breakfast and attempted to kill time. Again, patience is not one of my strong points. At 10:00 I called the Daniel's home again. Though Lee was not there, his wife said, "Come on out. He should be back very soon. "She had mentioned my call to him last night and he was expecting me. As I got a couple miles from his place, I found myself behind a new black Chevy one- ton dully pickup, loaded with lots of chrome with two large C.B. antennas whipping around. I followed the truck into the Daniel property. The truck pulled down to a shop, and as the driver got out, I pulled up behind him, parked and got out of my Ford and introduced myself. "Mr. Daniels my name is MM and I've just come back from Mexico. I've just completed this year's business with Jorge, and he suggested that you might be able to assist me with my logistics problem.

He looked me up and down and said, "How is that red- headed midget these days?"

"Very well, though he has had a growth spurt, side to side and top to bottom."

He stuck out his hand and said, "Lee Daniel. You want a beer?" He opened the ice chest in the back of his trunk.

As we shook hands, I replied, "Sure." I took a couple of sips and then we got down to business.

I explained I had a field of product that in a few weeks was going to be harvested and ready to pick up. I needed it brought over the border and preferably delivered to Dallas, or at least to a spot somewhere on this side. "How much weight are you talking about?" he asked. After I had told him the haul would be twenty-two to twenty- four thousand pounds, he asked, "Is this your first deal?"

"No, I have been doing this for eight years, flying my product over the border myself, but it is now so much weight that I do not want to make that many trips back and forth."

He understood, and this gave me some creditability. "I can haul two tons or a little more at a time," he said, "so it will still take a few trips. But we go back and forth several times a week regularly, so it will be no problem." Normally, this was when the real negations would start. Not this time. He had a fixed price of $5.00 a pound; the best I got from Lee was fifty cents more a pound, delivered to Dallas. The freight charge was to be paid in advanced of each delivery. The power was on his side, but at least I was reducing part of my tremendous risks, so it would be a win-win solution for each of us. There were several places he used for crossings: Matamoras to Brownville, Reynosa to McAllen, Pegras Negras to Eagle Pass, Cludad Acuna to Del Rio, and the two major crossing points of Juarez to El Paso and Nuevo Laredo to Laredo. Lee used all of them and knew which to use and when they were the busiest. I would not have been surprised if he had a few friends on the payroll who also were employed by a government agency. We talked about some other logistics, where he would like to unload and what equipment to have on hand to expedite the unloading. I left with his business card. He checked his phone every hour and he could be reached. I told him I would let him know the exact days and times, so he could work out his schedule.

I now had only one other problem. Where was I going to unload these shipments and then store this bulk? This was something I still had a little time to work on when I got home. I was actually ahead of time on my trip plan, so I decided to make an unplanned stop in Houston to visit Dusty Dan. I called and left him a message that I was in South Texas and heading his way if he had the time. Dan's products came in year- round and were always fresh if you could afford the prices.

Dust was a joy to visit. Besides his pot enterprise, he was a very interesting and smart guy. Rudy had once told me that he had a PhD. from Harvard and actually had been a professor at Rice University.

When I got to the Houston area and called him again, Dan answered this time. "I'm so glad you called. Meet me at a friend's home for dinner." He gave me the address and directions. He hung up before I got to ask him any questions, which was not like him, but I thought maybe he was in hurry or running late.

The friend turned out to be a lady friend, Ms. Lenora Evergreen, and the address turned out to be in a very wealthy part of Houston called River Oaks. When I knocked at the door Dan answered and was in a coat and tie and our host came up behind him soon after I stepped into her home. She was wearing some foreign designer silk frock with an expensive price tag, I'm sure. Her home was beautifully furnished with a lot of French provincial furniture, not my taste, but I could tell it was real, not knockoffs. The wood floors were also covered by fine quality Persian wool and fine Chinese silk antique rugs. I could sense she was not as glad to see me as Dan was, but she was very gracious. I was not dressed appropriately for formal dining and made a comment as such.

Dan replied, "Don't worry. Lenora is used to all different kinds of guests." Though the table was set for only two, one of the staff was adding a third, place setting, for me. I was dressed in a clean cowboy shirt, boots and jeans. As I put my hat and glasses down, I commented on her taste and surprised her with my knowledge of how well she had furnished her home. I explained, "I own an antique furnishings business in Dallas and go to Europe to buy several times a year." This seemed to relax her some; Lenora was so typical of the rich Texas women of the time, big hair, expensive clothes and jewelry. She had had plastic surgery done to make her late fifty-year-old body look ten years younger. She was chasing a dream and maybe Dan.

The dinner was presented on beautiful Wedgewood China. The crystal and silver were antiques and the flowers placed throughout the house completed the beautiful *Better Homes and Garden* look. We were served a gourmet meal. The first course consisted of an artichoke salad with light oil and vinegar dressing. The second course was a cold tomato soup followed by the main course of veal stuffed with crab meat and covered with a light lemon sauce. The sides were asparagus and roasted red potatoes. To top all of that rich food, the dessert was flaming baked Alaska. Three different wines were served during the meal with cognac or brandy after dinner. After a meal like that I kept waiting for someone to come out of the kitchen to ask for a charitable or political donation. All in all, it was nice, but the whole evening was uncomfortable because I was stuffed and wasted. Dan used my being a guest from out of town as an excuse to get us both out of there early. I followed Dan home slowly; I did not want a DWI. I think Dan had used me so he could get out of a romantic evening that he was not up for.

I ended up going to sleep at Dan's shortly after we got to his place and woke up the next morning with a terrible hangover and bad case of the runs. He was really going to owe me big time for that favor. We both took showers, and I drank a couple cups of tea with aspirin. We went to a little greasy spoon he knew and even though I was not that hungry, I ate some pancakes.

I called Tina from a pay phone at the grille to let her know I would be home that night. Then we went back to Dan's so he could show me his newest products. He selected a dark-colored bud from Africa. I took only two hits, and I was gone. I could hardly move my body, and the next five hours just seemed to float by. I know we listened to some Eric Clapton and Paul McCarthy's *Band on the Run* album. We had periods when we just chilled, saying nothing for hours. Then one of us would make a comment about something and we would break out in laughter to the point my cheeks hurt. This was some very, very heavy smoke. By three o'clock I was finally able to move and get myself together enough to head back home. I had made a purchase of several thousand dollars' worth of products, but not any of what we had smoked that morning. I personally do not enjoy such an intense high. What I imagine smoking opium must be like without the dream.

I finally got back home in time for dinner and found a very enthusiastic Tina. You would have thought I had been gone a month, not a few days, but I was not complaining. As we ate dinner, Tina excitedly told me of meeting a lady from the Lakewood Preservation League. "She said, we are just the right business this neighborhood needed and signed me up for the next meeting. I'll probably be able to get us new contacts, don't you think?"

"That's great T." I'm thinking, she's already thinking about ours and us. This group is promoting preservation, I did not see any big rallies or protest marches in their future for a bigger, better, "Keep Lakewood Original, movement." Their messages were not of social changes, I hope. After that news I needed a smoke, so I pulled out some hydroponically grown marijuana that I had gotten from Dusty that afternoon. This smoke was incredible. It gave me energy and a lift, which I was going to need as my lady was in a very passionate mood. We made like long lost lovers. I slept like the dead that night and woke up the next morning full of energy ready to conquer the world.

I was glad to be back in a familiar routine. I contacted a couple of commercial realtors to explain the *prerequisites* for the new storage space I was seeking. I needed a loading dock. I really needed two different places, one for furniture storage and the other for my green Mexican product.

The Little Oaks business had really picked up over the last few weeks since Tina had started. I was approached by the property owner who wanted to know if I would be interested in leasing the space next door as he thought the vintage clothing business was going to close. I met with the owner and Tina, and I checked out the space. Though it was about the same size as our current space, it would bring an extra bathroom and an area that would be perfect for building out for Tina's massage work. If we could keep the increase in business, it would easily pay for itself. I made a verbal commitment to take the space if the current tenant left. We still had to work out a new lease, but the owner would be happy if his building would not be empty.

Over the next few weeks I looked with realtors at maybe a dozen different properties for the warehouse space, but nothing seemed to fit my needs. Finally, I started driving around the area I had chosen but I had not looked at before. It took only forty-five minutes to find the right property. The building had a large covered loading dock in the back which ran the length of the building. Two spaces were twenty feet by fifty feet each, and a third was 5,000 square feet. Each one had its own roll-up doors in the back and a small office and showroom in the front of each space with front doors. There was not a lot of parking out front, but I did not need much.

I contacted the owner and met with him the next day. The large space which was what I was most interested in had clean floors; the warehouse portion was finished with insulation and sheet rock walls. The roof had skylights with security steel bars to prevent break-ins. The owner told me one of the overhead gas heaters worked well, but the other one needed repair or replacement. I would need some kind of climate control if I was going to store the wood furniture there, so that would be a consideration. I still would need some storage space for my marijuana, but I could find it somewhere else.

We were discussing the rental cost of the big space when out of the blue he asked, "Mr. Gold, if you would consider leasing the whole center, I would make you a good deal." He had been storing some of his own junk in one of the spaces; the center space had a roof leak, but the office was dry. The last space was in good shape and was where he currently stored his stuff. I got the whole building for only $300 more a month but had to take care of fixing things as needed. There was a lot of **needed.**

Rodger had been puttering into a legal business of his own. He had found a source of clean, empty wooden spools, the kind that cable and wire came on, and he was building patio furniture, which he sold to bars and restaurants for their outdoor seating. He was not getting rich, but it kept him out of most trouble. He had come by the Little Oak a few weeks earlier to see if I was going to need him this summer and, of course, to ask if I could front him with some product. If it had been anyone but Rodger, I would not have even thought about it, but I knew he would not leave me short. "I'll work you a deal on the new buds, but I'll have to get back to you on what I might need you to do later."

I set up a separate corporation for handling my business leases and the new store's property; it was to be another way for me to take legal income from the business. If Rodger was in for the deal, the new corporation would sublease him the end space, and I would store the Mexican inventory down there. It would give me a little distance between businesses but allow me to be close, but not too close.

I met Rodger for lunch that Friday and then showed him the space and went over the plan. "You can use the center warehouse space to store you're finished and unfinished furniture, and we will put the pot in the end space. You can display the patio and bar furniture in the front in the unused office." The only problem would be the odor that would emanate from the pot. I had an idea of buying coffee beans in sacks and placing them around and on top of the tarp covering the stash, all of which was to hopefully cover the smell. Rodger went for the idea and now I seemed to have most of my bases covered.

By the time the shipping containers started coming in from Europe, I had the new warehouse ready. I had a place to store items that needed work, and I wanted to move some inventory around from store to store. As I was buying higher quality items, I wanted to move some of the lesser quality pieces to Little Nut or to the warehouse. I had hired some day laborers to help unload and distribute items to the different stores. With the new inventory and rearranged pieces at the Little Oak, both stores had a fresh new look.

Rodger had moved his spool furniture business into his new space and was working on manufacturing, which he did by himself. He knew not to tell his friends or pot customers where to find him. His furniture customers were restricted to the front room whenever one came by to check out the finished products in person instead of by photograph.

The first load of Mexican was due the second weekend of September. I had made an arrangement with Lee and had made calls to my buyers to make sure we were all on the same page. Everything was going too smoothly, that worried me. I'm always looking for the other shoe to drop. Warily I went to a couple banks where I stored my cash anyway. I couldn't just put hundreds of thousands of dollars in my pocket or bury it in the backyard and that much cash always makes me uncomfortable. It was like having unprotected sex with someone you just met in a bar; more bad things than good things can happen.

I flew to Mexico. Alejandro met me at the dirt road by the field where we began weighing bricks and bundles. By the time Lee arrived, most of the weighing and inventorying of the shipment was complete. All we had to do was a load. The inside of Lee's trailer looked normal at first glance, but he had a double-front interior piece that could be pulled out so contraband items could be stored between the walls. This part of the trailer sat over the truck's drive wheels. Someone would have to measure the inside and then compare it to the outside dimensions to tell the difference. Lee would pick up a load of watermelons after we were done, and it was highly unlikely that he would be asked to unload the melons for the border crossing. Timing was important, and Lee knew the best time to cross in each city he used. The day of the week also played a part in his decision. He had it figured out and all I had to do was pay him.

After Lee had left, I flew back to San Antonio to meet with my man Rudy. He insisted that I go out to dinner with his family. His sister owned a great hole-in-the-wall Tex-Mex restaurant that mostly catered to Hispanics and a few Anglos who knew of this hidden gem. Rosa would not let me leave until I had sampled almost the entire menu, so I left stuffed. Her cooking embodied the love of family and that made it taste extra delicious.

After dinner, Rudy dropped his family off, and we headed to my motel. We relaxed, lit up a J, back into his old routine. He told me some new jokes and had me laughing so hard I almost peed myself. As we sat in his car and talked business, I found that his, like mine, was growing almost too fast to keep up. We talked prices and compared what we felt the market could bear. "Max, I have a New York client who was selling his pounds for $500 each and is doubling his order every time he comes to town, and when I raise my price, it never bothers him."

"My product will be picked up in the next few days," I answered.

"Really?" responded Rudy. "Mine will not be ready for at least a couple of weeks, and then I have to get it across the border. How much will you charge me for, say 1,500 pounds?"

"Oh, now the shoe's on the other foot," I grinned. "I'll tell you what. If you can pick it up in Big D, I'll let you have it for…"

Before I had the figure out of my mouth, he said, "Too high."

Besides the business of the sale, we agreed to raise our prices $50 a pound more than we had originally intended, except to the few clients from which I had already given a price.

Rudy looked seriously straight-faced at me and asked, "Do you think the government would consider this price fixing?"

"Oh then maybe we should reconsider doing it," I came back. We broke out laughing. I don't know any comedian who could break me up like Rudy. I went up to my room but did not sleep very well. I was too excited thinking about the next few months. It always gives me such a rrrusssh.

I got up early the next morning and headed back up the concrete ribbon of Interstate 35. The old Ford was just south of Waco when I noticed a buxom, blond lady and a little girl on the side of the highway, standing beside a pickup truck that had a cargo trailer like mine. Smoke billowed out of the front grill of the truck and from under the hood. It had just started to rain. I usually don't stop to help fellow motorists, but I thought, "What if that was Tina?" I turned around and pulled up behind them. I got out and asked if I could give them a lift to the nearest service station. The woman said, "I cannot leave the truck." The little girl started to cry as the rain began to pick up.

"Look, get in my truck. The heater is working if you need it, and I'll check out your truck and see if I can fix it." I popped the hood and was greeted with the smell of steam and burnt oil. One quick look and it was apparent what had happened. The water pump belt broke. With no water pump, the engine heats up, and the red light comes on. The lady had ignored the light, so the motor had seized up. This truck was not going anywhere on its own. I climbed back into my cab, wet and cold. "That truck is not going anywhere," I explained as simply as I could what had happened. When I mentioned the red light, she put a guilty look on her face; then sudden fear crossed her whole being. I gave her a few options.

"I can't leave the trailer," she slipped. Now, I understood. It was the load that was important. She had mentioned that they were coming from San Antonio on the way to Lake Worth, just on the north-west side of Fort Worth.

"Look, let me hook it up to my truck. We can find some place to make a call to whoever you need to call. It's not a good idea for you to stay here with your little girl.

"Oooo-Kaaa," she finally said. I got back out and in just a few rained soaked minutes we were back on the road heading north. As we drove the next sixty miles, her story came out. "My name is Tammy, Tammy Cox and this is Angie." Tammy was an exotic dancer and her boss, Sonny, was allowing her to pay off a loan by making this trip. Who was going to stop a lady with a little girl? That was a good plan, except for the unexpected.

"Tammy, do you know what is in the trailer?" I asked.

"Are you a cop?" she asked.

"No, but I have a pretty good idea what's inside and why your boss got you and Angie to make the drive."

"I really don't know," she replied to my question, "but it must be important or valuable because Sonny was very specific about not letting the truck and trailer out of my sight." Angie had been very quiet all this time, but as we got to the I-35 split, left to Fort Worth, right to Dallas, she started to complain about being hungry and needing to potty. This was as good a reason as any to stop and have Tammy make her call. I took the phone from her when I heard all the screaming from the other end.

"If you will calm down and listen to me, this can go very smoothly with no problems," I told Sonny and then gave him the exit number and the name of the diner where we were parked.

It only took Sonny and one of his guys about an hour to find us. We had just finished eating when they both walked in and up to our booth. Both men looked tough but were not carrying any guns as far as I could see. They were heavily tattooed and looked like fighting was a sport in which they excelled. I got up, extended my hand and introduced myself as MM. He took my hand and shook it. Sonny introduced himself and just the two of us sat down. I explained what I had found when I had pulled over to check on Tammy and Angie. "True to her word, Tammy would not leave without the trailer, so I hooked it up and brought them here."

"I hope she made it worth your while," he said with a sadistic smile on his face. "Did you look inside?"

"No, I figured what her load was when she told me where she was coming from, the time of year and everything, but this is your trailer and it's none of my business, but I also deal in the commodity and maybe in the future you might have a need for my product." We went outside and continued to talk as his companion hooked the trailer to the new truck that the guys were driving. I sold him some weight, and saved him $20 per pound, and as I was delivering, saved him road time.

Sonny had done two tours of duty in Vietnam as a Ranger and now owned the "Witches Tit" bar where Tammy worked. His clients were mostly current military guys but he was selling pounds to fellow vet friends. "If you placed an order now, I will hold it for four months and will sell it to you in as little as fifty pounds loads."

"How do I reach you?" he asked.

"Give me your contact number. When things are ready, I will contact you from a payphone. It's my way or none at all," I explained.

"Why did you stop for Tammy, MM?" Sonny asked.

"It was just a feeling and I always follow my gut." We shook hands good bye and I told him he owed Tammy a bonus for doing such a good job for him. Tammy and Angie came over and gave me a hug and a kiss on my cheek. This was a great feeling, especially when the beneficiary was a fellow member of the Brotherhood of Smoke.

After leaving the dinner, my first stop was the Little Nut to check in with my girl. She asked what took so long and why I had lipstick on my cheek. Tina and I had not been together very long, but she knew me well enough to know I was a one-woman man and not a player. However, I did have to explain, "I have been rescuing two fair damsels in distress, and the kiss on my cheek was my reward."

"Is that *all* you got for your effort?" Tina asked with a smirk.

"No, I actually got a new customer as well," I answered.

Tina then changed the subject and began filling me in on what was happening in the stores. The landlord had called, and the next-door space was definitely going to be available at the end of the next month. Did we still want the space?

"Do you still want studio space for your massage clients?" I asked.

"Yes!" was her quick reply. Then she kissed me, stuck her tongue into my ear and then and whispered, "I will give you my own just reward tonight."

Lee had the trailer backed up to the end space at the dock when I got there in the early morning hours. I opened the overhead door, and we began loading dollies and two-wheelers full of heady-scented bricks. We had the load off the truck, stacked and covered with tarps and bags of coffee in less than an hour and a half. I paid him for the next load, and we set up another pick- up time for the end of next week. The warehouse was beginning to have the smell of coffee, and I was hungry. I took a random brick home and then headed for a pay phone to see who was ready with cash in hand for the 1974 fall harvest.

My Oklahoma City people, and the Tulsa group were more than ready, so I made arrangements to load up and meet them Friday. When I called Dirk's cowboy bar, his bartender brother-in-law answered. I asked Dirk. He said "Hold on MM." Instead of Dirk's voice, I got his wife Dorothy. She was all freaked out and said she needed to meet with me.

"Meet me at noon at the park just down the street from the bar," I said and hung up. I had only met her once and hoped I would recognize her. Dirk had involved her in the business, which I felt was wrong, but that was his operation. I parked down the street early and walked to the park. There was something in her voice that put me on alert, so before I sat down, I checked the area out, scanning for people who looked out of place or were in cars but not eating lunch. I didn't get any bad feelings or warning alerts, so I sat and waited. I watched as Dorothy drove up to check for anyone following her. Maybe I was being overly cautious, but it was better to be safe than sorry.

She got out of her car and joined me at a picnic table. She told me, "Dirk was arrested last week for assaulting a guy at the bar who had been causing trouble and would not leave. The other guy threw the first punch. "The charges are bogus," she said, "but he has been investigated by the police for robberies, a burglary and drug dealing lately." Now she really had my attention. They had picked him up on the street and questioned him for eight hours before they allowed him a phone call. Before I could get the money to a bail bondsman, he was locked up in a holding cell with several other guys, he got into a fight with one of them and was stabbed several times, sending him to the hospital." She also told me, that "There had been some strange things happening at the bar lately. A phone guy came by to check the service, which we have not had any problems with and two other guys who are not regulars showed up asking questions about my brother and trying to sell him gold jewelry or swap some for pot. All of this has just started over the last few weeks."

"Do you have an attorney?" I asked.

"Only the one we use for business," she said.

"First call this guy," as I gave her Abe, "the Barbarian", Blend's business card. "Tell him I sent you. Tell him exactly what you told me. Be totally honest with him, and he will handle the rest. He can probably get the charges dropped. Ask him if he can get someone to check your bar and home phone for electronic bugs. He can find out through the back doors what is really going on. If the law has any investigation or evidence on Dirk, then at least you will know what you are dealing with. Okay? He is not cheap, but he is good, and cheap is not what you want when you are going against the government."

"I still have the cash for our order despite everything Max and we still needed to make the deal so as not to lose our customers. My brother and I will take up the slack."

"Look at this time with all the heat, let's see what the attorney can find out first. I promised you I will hold you- all's order, and, in a few weeks, I will contact you and we can go from there." I understood her need, but it seemed Dirk had pissed someone off and was now probably on someone's radar or at least someone's fishing expedition, and I did not want to be caught up in someone's net by accident or on purpose,**" If you don't want fleas, don't sleep with dogs."** I watched her leave and waited to see if she was followed. Nope. Not today.

I loaded my trailer for my first two deliveries in over seven months. The juice was on, and I was high just from the anticipation. I left early Friday morning and was about twenty-five miles south of Oklahoma City when I ran over something in the road. The truck cleared the debris, but the trailer's axles, which sat lower, caught the trash. The trailer started to shake and weave, almost causing a collision with a passing car in the next lane, which honked as it passed me. I was just lucky I was able to slow down enough to keep control of both truck and the trailer. When I finally stopped on the side of the highway and got out of the truck. I was not happy with what I found. The first axle was bent back, making the wheel look like a bowed cowboy leg. The second axle was even worse. The trailer must have jumped when the first axle hit the debris, and when it landed, the second axle hit the trash. This axle was broken into two pieces, leaving the tires to V in. This could not be fixed with duct tape or the baling wire that I had in my toolbox.

I found myself in the same position Tammy was in only a few days earlier. I did not want to leave the trailer on the side of the road to go and get help, and I did not know if I was going to have to unload the trailer to get it fixed. If I rented another trailer, I did not like the idea of unloading and reloading on the side of an interstate. I was running all this through my mind when, out of the blue, my own white- knight. A young wrecker driver pulled up. He got out to look under the truck and then the trailer and asked if the truck was okay. I replied, "Yes, it's just the trailer."

"Well," he said, "I can put some dollies under her and tow you wherever you want, to a station or repair shop," I asked him if there was anyone, he would recommend that could get on it in a hurry and do a good job. "My Uncle Bill is a welder and does some trailer work. He is good. I could give him a call."

"Make it happen," I said, and I began thinking this might work out if I don't have to unload the trailer. He told me that if I wanted, he could pull the trailer back to his storage yard and Bill could work there. I liked this better every minute. "How much is this going to cost me?" I asked, afraid of the answer.

"One hundred fifty for the tow, and thirty-seven fifty a day for storage, will that work for you?"

Expensive, but not outrageous, "Let's do it," I said and moved to the back of the truck to unhitch it. I pulled out of the way as the wrecker pulled into my place. He had the two sets of dollies under the axle in no time, and I followed him down the road. He exited, crossed over the interstate, and then drove down the service road to an old country road. We were on it for several miles until we came to a sheet metal fence with razor wire on the top. This was perfect. I could not have asked for a better location to do business. Now all I hoped for was for his uncle to come and not need to empty the trailer. If the kid was interested in making some extra cash, I might have really lucked out.

His Uncle Bill was waiting for us when we arrived and helped situate the trailer. He got under the cargo van and took down part numbers. "These should not be too hard to find," he said. "But it might be tomorrow before I can get the parts unless you want me to just jerry -rig it. The cost will be about the same."

"Order the parts and see if we can get this done today. If not, tomorrow it will be." Doing it right the first time is better than a half-ass job that would need to be redone later and in the meantime it might break down on the road again before I could get it done right.

After Uncle Bill left, I asked Johnny Cee, the young driver, if he would be interested in making a total of a $1,000 on this project. "Who do I have to kill?" he asked.

I laughed and said, "Nobody, but I have some business to conduct over the next several hours, and I need to be sure that I will not be interrupted here."

"For a grand, you can have this place all day and all night for all I care." We had our deal, and I use of his office phone and made two phone calls. My Oklahoma City client could be here in forty minutes or less, but my Tulsa man was going to need a few hours to get a trailer and drive down. I promised him a price break for his inconvenience.

I opened the back of the trailer and found a mess. Though nothing was torn up, the load had shifted, and I would have to inventory the bricks. Most of the time, my buyers did not want to reweigh each brick and would randomly pick out several, and I would bring out the scales and weigh them. Most were already inventoried, and I went by the poundage on the packaging. If I ran into a discrepancy, unless it was something that ran into many bricks, I wrote it off as the cost of doing business. I always made it right with my customers though.

My Oklahoma City guy came. I was closing the metal gates while he was inspecting his load. We weighed ten random bricks, and he opened a couple to check the contents. He then rolled a few joints and lit one. His partner lit the other, and we loaded his van. They left loaded in more than one way. I found some jacks and put them under my trailer, took an air wrench and started to unbolt the axles so Bill would have that much less to do. I had one set totally off and the second set is almost done when my Tulsa guy knocked on the metal doors. He was getting more of the load than my other customer, and he was a bit picky and paranoid. I was in no hurry, and we were in a very secure location, so I let him take his time and weigh as many as he wanted. After an hour, when not even half the load had been weighed, he gave up and settled for my numbers. I was saving him over $500, so in the long run he was happy. He also left very stoned. My customers are generally happy with my product, and I rarely get complaints about the quality of smoke or the high that it gives them.

I had both axles free and pulled out with the help of a chain and my truck by the time Johnny returned late that afternoon. He told me Uncle Bill had ordered the new axle and he would be picking it up in the morning. I should be back on the road by noon. He noticed the trailer doors were open, airing out and that the load was gone. I asked him if he smoked pot. "Sure do," he said.

"Well, here is your $1,000 cash as promised and a lid of fresh Mexican. Enjoy. I'm going to find a motel room and will see you in the morning."

I left him one happy camper. I was happy the day was over, and I had made it through another disaster. I called Tina from the motel's pay phone and told her I had had some mechanical difficulties but should be home tomorrow after I got the trailer repaired.

Uncle Bill was busily working on the trailer when I got to the wrecker yard the next morning, and he had me back on the road by 11:00. I paid him in cash which made him happy. Johnny was out working the road, so Uncle Bill thanked me for both of them and smiled. "If you need our services any time or the use of the yard just calls, it is yours to use." I gathered Johnny had shared some information and maybe some smoke with Uncle Bill. Most importantly, the trailer pulled straight and smoothly down the road.

I stopped in Sherman, a small town just inside the Texas- Oklahoma border, to fuel up the truck. As I was heading home. I noticed movement in the back of a pickup truck parked next door in a small strip shopping center. My curiosity got the better of me, so I slowly drove by. There appeared to be an eight or nine-year-old boy and his grandfather sitting on lawn chairs next to an old farm truck and a sign on the tailgate that read, "Puppies for Sale." I pulled in next to them and went out to investigate. I really had not been looking for a pet, but one glance and I was hooked. Inside the truck bed were eight golden retriever puppies, each one more adorable than the next. The little boy told me, "They are only six weeks old and not potty-trained." The pups were running around the bed jumping and chewing on each other and assorted trash in the back of the truck. I picked up several different ones but kept coming back to one large male that was very inquisitive and loving.

"How much are you asking for the pups?" I inquired.

The boy climbed into the back with the dogs and leaned over the tailgate and said into my ear, "These dogs and the father are farm dogs which make them like Lassie." The kid was a natural-born salesman. He then started asking me questions. "Do you live on a farm? Because these type dogs need to be able to run around a lot and they like to swim." He wanted to know how many kids I had and if they were boys because these types of dogs need boys to look after them. He was a real treat.

I explained, "I do not live on a farm, but I do have a large fenced-in back yard, and I do not have any kids yet, but when I do, I will be sure to only order boys. I have a girlfriend and she will make sure he gets lots of attention and will be looked after when I was not around." I must have passed inspection because he allowed me to spend $150 for one of his dogs. The grandfather was standing by to take the money, and he took my name and address to send me the dog's AKC registration papers and he made sure I understood the feeding instructions.

My new best friend "Wally" and I went back on the road. He wanted to play, began to chew on my arm, and then my watch band. He finally settled for my leather belt. The last hour of the trip he just slept with his head in my lap.

When we got back to Dallas, my first stop was to a pet supply store. I purchased dog food, a brush, a collar, bowls for food and water, a leash and what turned out to be Wally's favorite chew toy, a small stuffed squeaky toy that looked something like a squirrel. I called Tina and reached her at the Little Nut. "Hey T we are going to have a dinner guest."

"Who?"

I simply replied, "Surprise," and we went on discussing store business.

"And Max, please pick up an order of plants from the greenhouse and bring them by the store. Oh by the way, do I need to fix anything special for our guest tonight?

"See you in a bit," I replied and hung up. The next stop was to the greenhouse and the Big Oak. When I put Wally's new collar around his neck, he shook his head and rolled over trying to get it off. He was cute to watch. He finally settled down after I spoke to him and started to praise him. I needed to show him how a good dog behaves and what unacceptable behavior was. I have had dogs before. A smart dog will learn fast and live to serve their people. Giving praise to my dogs was as good as getting a treat. They loved both but needed the human's love more than anything.

I attached the leash to his collar and lifted him down to the ground. Off we went exploring. The greenhouse was full of lots of different smells, and Wally was going to check each one out. Finally, he got into a walking rhythm with me, and the longer he was by my side, the less I had to use the leash. I could tell I had another smart dog.

I took Wally into Helen's and Frances' office to show him off. Helen was out, but Frances got off the phone, he dropped to the floor and scooped poor Wally up in his arms. "Where did you find this handsome beast?" Frances asked.

"I bought him off a farmer and his grandson in Sherman as a surprise for Tina."

"Oh, she is going to love this cute little guy," Frances replied. Then he told me that he had a strong bite on the two eighteenth-century French writing desks that I brought back from England after the hoax and threat incident that still makes my staff laugh to recall. I had been sitting on those two pieces because they were exact, matching pieces with custom woodwork and hand carvings on the sides and legs. The top's exquisite designs had been created exclusively for Napoleon. These two tables were worth double, maybe two and a half, what I had in them, so I was taken back when Frances spoke of them. When he told me what he was selling them for, I almost lost my breath! We would make over 400%.

"If this goes through, you will have a little bonus due you." I slapped him on the back, asked him to keep an eye on Wally for a few minutes, and headed toward the cash register. I put $5,000 cash in the till and made up a receipt for Wally Jones.

Over the years I had found ways to filter cash money received or cash paid out for inventory into the business; most people try to do just the opposite. The drug business is a cash-only business. I couldn't just deposit large sums of cash in a bank account without showing how I got the cash legally. So, to run cash through my legitimate furniture or plant businesses, I needed to write a phony sales receipt and put the cash in the till. In several cities, after I had finished my deliveries and had an empty trailer, it was my habit to go by various antique and fine furniture stores in the area where I'd l buy items that I knew we could move at one of the stores, pay cash using a fake name. I sometimes paid more than I should just because I liked the item or knew it would be an easy sale, resulting in a smaller margin. I could then pull some of the profits out of business, both real and injected money. I had to pay taxes on this money, but I could show an income, get credit, doing the things legally that I needed to do.

The girls in the green house had loaded Tina's order and my buddy and I were off again. We arrived at the Little Nut just about quitting time. Tina was helping a client load a side table. I jumped out to help, forgetting about Wally. He also jumped out of the truck to follow me. I grabbed Tina's end of the table, and she looked down just in time to catch Wally peeing on the side of my leg. Maybe he wasn't so smart. I scolded him, so he ran straight over to Tina and sat right between her legs. Both Tina and the customer laughed, and I have to admit he did look cute. "I can see I have more training work to do than I had first thought with you Wally." She reached down to pick him up and he kissed her face like he had just found his new mother. It was love at first sight for both of them. From the first day if Tina did not take him to the store with her in the mornings, he would howl all day. On rare occasions, he might grace me with his companionship; every so often I would take him on a pot delivery run. On those occasions I liked to see how Wally interacted with my clients. He was a very good judge of people with good instincts. Once, when Wally kept barking at a customer, I had to put him in the truck. But Wally just kept barking at the customer, causing me to proceed cautiously. When I checked the tally, I had failed to include several pounds that he had loaded, without my knowledge. I never dealt with this customer again. If Wally didn't like him, I took his advice.

I went back to unloading the new plant inventory while Tina sold three of the new plants, I had brought with me to our last customer of the day. "Maxie, I'm so glad about my choice of dinner guest and I love your surprise for me. You are a good man, though I like you better without the straw hat and those big mysterious glasses. I want to see those dark eyes of yours. "Now, catch me, if you can." Off she ran with Wally eagerly running, tail wagging behind her, leaving me in third position in this chase.

1975

President Ford is forced to make huge financial decisions after the unemployment rate hits 9.2% and the city of New York is facing bankruptcy. Leaving him no other choice but to grant a loan for 2.3 million dollars to the city.

President Ford proclaimed the United States is officially in a recession.

Bill Gates and Paul Allen developed the basic program for the Altaic 8800 which came out.

Jaw's was scaring us at the movies, and X-teamster Jimmy Hoffa disappears, but Patty Hurst is found and arrested for armed robbery.

The big fight is between Sony's Beta max format, or the rival JVC's , VH S recorder/player.

John Mitchell, John Ehrlichman, and H.R.Halderman, the last of the Watergate conspirator are sentenced for conspiracy and obstruction of justice.

One day when Wally was about eighteen months old, a male customer came into the Little Nut. He became very loud and demanding while haggling with Tina over the price of an old queen sleigh bed and two dressers. "I guess he thought he could intimidate me," she told me as she told the story. "But before I could respond, Wally faced the fellow with a snarling grin. And before the guy knew it, our ninety-five-pound gentle golden retriever stood up and put one of his paws on each side of this guy's shoulders, growling and baring his teeth while at the same time moving the now freaked -out customer back toward the door. The guy slowly backed out the door and promptly fled, Wally was wagging his tail and he had the biggest smile on his face. And guess what? The dude, he did call back the next day to apologize to me for his demeanor. He gave me his MasterCard number for the pieces and gladly paid both the quoted price and the delivery fee without further argument."

Over the next few months, I went to Mexico twice, Houston three times, Austin four times, San Antonio four times; and twice each to Shreveport, Baton Rouge, Fayetteville, and Little Rock, and in October of 1975 I made two trips to Lake Worth to visit Sonny. I also did finally agree to meet Dirk's wife Dorothy out in the country to do the deal as I had promised. The location gave me a view where I could see for miles in all directions; the view was interrupted only by a wooded area in the middle area naturally protected from aerial view. I got there early to be vigilant and when we did make the cash/ pot swap it did go smoothly and quite quickly, she just was grateful. The problem for me though Dorothy had brought her son instead of her brother. I was not happy with this arrangement, but Dirk was still recovering and couch- ridden. The boy was in his early teens, and I really did not think she should expose him to this.

"I tell you, Dorothy, I do not feel comfortable with Dirk putting you in the middle of our business in the first place. Now your teenage son is involved. It's not acceptable. I'm sorry but cannot do business with you guys again." I left as soon as we completed our business. Yes, I would miss Dirk's business, but as it turned out, it was a wise decision. In less than two years I was to learn that Dirk had been busted for selling and possessing cocaine, and another time busted for marijuana distribution brought on by his son's arrest for dealing pot and storing it in his locker at his high school. Dirk was also arrested for being part of a group which imported cocaine from Columbia. He had become flashy with his money and the family was living large while his new business associates were doing likewise. The whole group drew the attention of the wrong people, both Federal and State agencies. They also must have stepped on the toes of at least one of their competitors who were probably behind Dirk's stabbing in the first place. The local news was all over this for a few days, then nothing. Dirk made a plea and was sentenced to ten years in Huntsville State Prison. To say I was worried is an understatement, but in the end, he took his time and never rolled over or gave up the name of customers or supplier to my knowledge. He followed the unwritten dealers' code*." You do the crime you do the time!"*

One morning, the storm of Rodger rolled in all upset and mad. "Dammit, Max, someone broke in my mom's garage last night and took the twenty-eight- pound stash that I was to deliver today."

"Well, it was probably one of your friends or maybe someone has been following you. Keep an eye out for someone you know who starts sporting a new car or are wearing jewelry that he can't afford." I also told him, "You need to start watching to see and make sure you are not being followed back to the warehouse. We certainly do not need anyone to know where the motherlode is being stored." He agreed, but I could tell it was really bothering him. It was more than the money lost. **"Beware of your friends not your enemies."** As it turned out, one of his oldest friends from Denton showed up a few weeks later driving a year-old, loaded Ford Pickup. He told Rodger his dad won it in a card game and gave it to him. Rodger called his friend's father.

"Look Rodger" he said, "I cannot afford to piss my money away on gambling, even if I knew how, which I don't. I have no idea where the damn truck came from, stolen for all I know. "Rodger never accused his friend directly, but when they got into an argument over a food bill, Rodger ran him off. We talked one afternoon over lunch. He was earnestly devastated and disappointed in the so-called friend's betrayal.

"Rodger," I said, "a true friend is really hard to find. When you have one, hold on to them." We both felt ours was one of those friendships.

"Yeah Man, we go back to grade school, and we have had our shining moments. Remember the chickens?" We both had a big grin at that memory.

I was done with most of my deliveries before the first of the year. Dusty needed some of my Mexican for a few of his regular clients, so I planned to make a quick run and drive down to Houston. Before I left though, Rodger asked if I would come with him to deliver fifty pounds just outside of Houston. These were people he had dealt with last year and he wanted a side man. We took his truck, and I don't know why, but I was not getting a positive vibe about this trip. We exited I/45 just outside of Houston in a small town called Spring. We drove through the small, old-time downtown area with the big window store fronts and then down several tree- lined country roads. Rodger seemed to know where he was going. We finally pulled into a pasture and parked next to a small patch of trees, just down from a couple-years-old black Mercury sedan. Two biker guys covered with tattoos got out. The driver was a short swarthy man with a tree trunk of a neck sprouting from his shoulders, his oil-black hair, hanging long past his sun-blocking shoulders. The passenger was a tall thin man with an ugly red scar running from one corner of this mouth to just below his right ear. They moved like they had a mission. No pleasantries they had come for business. Scarface was bitching about having to wait on us as Rodger exited the truck to meet them. I waited and observed from the cab everything routine, as Caveman rolled a joint and smoked it by himself. Rodger asked, "Well, whaddya think?" Two thumbs up were the answer.

The scar-faced guy brought out a balance beam scale from the trunk to check the bricks. They weighed a couple of them and were tallying the purchase as Scarface strolled back to the Mercury's open trunk. I was still watching all this unfold in the mirrors of the truck. Like a slow-motion dream, I saw the tall, scared freak bend over. As he rose up this time he was holding, unmistakably, a 12- gauge double barrel shot gun with a cut-down handle and shortened barrel. Suddenly, the Neanderthal is outside my window pointing a .38 caliber revolver in my face. Finally, he had something to say," Geet out of the fuucking truck, assshoole, an geeet busy loading myyyy shit."

As I exited from the truck cab, I felt a body and mind rush of adrenaline, yet all the activity and motion seemed to slow down to microseconds. I 'm thinking, *'Max you might not live through this day. What will Tina, my folks, and all these other people think?'* Stupid to be worrying about what someone else would think at the moment of my possible death, but I couldn't control where my thoughts went. My legs felt like they were wearing concrete shoes; just walking took extreme effort. As we approached the truck, Rodger climbed into the truck bed and positioned his back against the rear window of the cab.

Slim backed the sedan up closer to the tailgate but was soon back with his shotgun pointing at us. He moved behind his partner. Cautiously, I reached into the bed of the truck to gather a handful of bricks from the back of the stack. With my body lying prone across the bricks, I looked up just in time to watch as Rodger surreptitiously reached behind his back and pulled out a huge gun. As if he was playing a part in a movie, Rodger raised the cannon, fired two shots over my head and horizontally lying body. I quickly turned around to see who Rodger fired at, only to see where one of the shots landed, on the forehead of the shotgun-toting scarred-faced man. A large area of the front lob and most of the back of his head was missing, red and white brain matters exposed, and blood everywhere. His body involuntarily reacts by pulling the trigger of his cut-off double barrel shot gun, blowing a big hole in the backside of his soon to be dead partner.

My attention had been on Greasy, so I had seen firsthand what the spray from his partner's shotgun blast did to him as the multiple tiny shots invaded this man-tree's body. His eyes bulged almost out of his head, he opened his mouth open to scream, but no sound came out, only dark red, bubbling blood. He dropped to his knees and then fell over, the tree cut down. All this I saw in a min-moment.

I froze for a split second; then survivor mode kicked in. I jumped out of the truck bed, yanking Rodger with me and pulling the gate up in one smooth move. One push and Rodger got into the truck cab and me into the passenger seat. We flew back the way we had come. My concern was that the artillery noise would draw attention and then someone would come to investigate. The sky which had been gray all day turned to hard rain. There is not a lot of traffic in these small towns normally, but because of the rain, we never saw any other vehicles. No way was I in the mood to see Dusty, so I pointed Rodger back up Interstate 45 north and only then did I finally let it all sink in. I kept hearing muffled words in my head, though it took me a few moments to realize that it was Rodger babbling. *"Did you see the short-lived smile on that cut face mother fucker just before my bullet ripped it off?" Those mother fucks thought they were going to rip me off. Fuck them. Nobody is going to rip me off or mess with me. I showed them didn't I, Max?"*

My thoughts are, why would he put himself through this, let alone me? Even if it was self-defense, I was beginning to feel used, and by Rodger of all people. I was totally drained out.

As we were heading north on Interstate 45, I looked to my right and saw that we were passing by the notorious Huntsville state prison. I could see many of the high chain link fences with their crown of sharp razor wire and concrete buildings with very few windows beyond. I exploded on Rodger. "How could you have done that? You could have shot me!" I screamed. "You could have missed, and they would have shot both of us and not thought twice about it. We can both end up right there." I pointed to the state prison. "It's one thing to get busted for pot, but for murder? This could be our home for a long time, or worse we could end up being fried by Old Sparky, is that what you want?" He knew that when I mentioned Sparky, it was the famous wooden electric chair that the state had used for many years to execute their death row inmates. "How stupid could you have been, Rodger? You must have known that those guys could be trouble!" I guess I was now responding to the adrenaline. I looked down to see that I was smearing blood and mixed body pieces and guts onto the truck seat and floorboard. We stopped at a roadside rest stop as the only other visitor was pulling out. I found an old red shop rag under the seat and asked Rodger for his gun. My hand shook as I set the gun on the rag covering my lap and began taking the firearm apart. The next few minutes were spent carefully rubbing the manufactured pieces free of fingerprints, one by one. Painfully and slowly, I moved out of the truck, taking the remaining cartridges and a few of the gun pieces with me. I walked through the rain to behind the building housing the restrooms which backed up to a wooded area, and with all my might threw each piece as far as I could in different directions.

I was now soaked and feeling despondent. Rodger restarted the truck, and we continued down the highway. We rode in the dark with only the lights on the dashboard and the sound of the windshield wipers going back and forth, clearing our view with each movement only to be replaced with more raindrops to be cleared. We rode in silence. What was there to say?

After we had driven halfway home, I saw a sign for a truck stop. "Rodger, pull in here, I needed to get out of these wet and stained clothes. Here's some cash, buy me a new pair of Levi's, and a baseball cap, along with a sweatshirt to replace my bloody and gut-covered clothes and a large blanket to cover this newly stained truck seat. And how is it Rodger that you have managed to come out of this melee without getting a single drop of the mess on you?" He just shrugged as he went off to shop. When he returned, I changed in the truck as we were driving back down the road. I took my old clothes, bundled them up and shoved them under the seat to deal with when I got back to Dallas. I had Rodger make only one more stop as we crossed over the Trinity River into Dallas, and that was to throw the last piece of the gun into the slow-moving, dark, murky water. Under my breath, I whispered, "May you find your way to hell."

When we got back to the warehouse, I let Rodger unload his truck. While he was doing that, I sprinkled paint thinner over my blood and death-stained clothes. I tried to burn that unholy mess out of existence in an old fifty-five-gallon drum out back behind the building in the alley. The fire incinerated the incriminating garments, but the images of that day had seared my conscience forever.

Even after smoking a joint, I was still so pissed and worked up that I knew I wasn't ready to face Tina, so I rented a motel room in town and called Dan, explaining something had come up, but that I would get back with him in a few days.

I waited until I knew Tina was at work the next morning to finally go home and change clothes. I found no mention of our encounter when I scanned the *Dallas Morning News*, and it wouldn't air on the local TV news until late that night when the story broke that two Dallas men were found shot to death in a field outside of Spring in what was thought to be a drug deal gone bad. Those two men could easily have been Rodger and me, so I was left with "what ifs?" but no answers.

I do not know what makes a man kill another man, but I suspect Rodger's primal instinct of kill or be killed was his self-preservation reaction. Though this was a deal that would have resulted in just a small profit, he was armed for conflict because he knew the risk was high. Why take such risks for so little reward? I also know some of the anger Rodger had was due to the betrayal of his friend who had ripped him off months earlier, and he had the hidden rage, that he had been carrying since 1963 and the death of his dad. At any rate, I neither wanted nor needed to become a part of anything like what happened yesterday.

It was a few weeks later before Rodger showed back up at the spool factory. "Hey buddy, you really need to try this Peruvian sugar, I just scored." He proceeded to snort the two lines of South American powder in front of me.

"Rodger, what the fuck are you doing, and why are you using cocaine now, are you crazy?"

"It is too good Max you really need to take a hit, plus I can keep it up all night long and keep my ladies happy. You remember the brunette with those really big tits? Well, she and two friends came over and…"

"Rodger, you are out of control. I love you Brother, but you are acting too dangerous, your wheels are coming off, you need some serious help. Let s talk some maybe get you some help, maybe dry you out, what do you say?"

"Screww yooou , Max! "

I have known Rodger since grade school; he is my closest friend. In some ways we were tighter than even Tina and I, but in a different way. "A guy's way," we had been through so much together and in each other's lives so long.

Obviously, Rodger's and my relationship became strained, and after that session our relationship ended at least for now. I could not have him around my family or businesses.

The death experience theirs and almost mine left me in a wash with emotions, I had to take off the rose -colored vision of my world, and see it for what it has become. And now left with the big decision am I going to have to start carrying a gun? If I carry a gun will I actually use it? This was not something you leave up to; we'll see when it comes up. I finally came to the decision, "No," short of defending my family against aggression, I just don't have it in me to take someone's life, certainly not over money or magic green vegetation.

The trip back down I-45 to Houston, to make my promised delivery to Dusty, was the longest, hardest, and even a bit apprehensive a trip, I have ever had. Especially when driving through Spring on I/45. My body tightened up and I got so nauseous that I had to pull over and visit my lunch. The only way I was going to get back into the reality of it was to face my demons and move forward. **"If you swim against the current, you cannot stop; you can either go forward or back."**

Of course, it did not hurt that when I got to Dan's, he had just gotten in some nicely wrapped Ti-sticks.

The work on the Little Nut's wall opening and Tina's massage space was almost done. She had selected green tones for her space which had a soothing effect on the environment. Along with Tina's massage table, we added a small stereo system to her new space. After hours I would often go out back, smoke a joint and use her studio just to relax to the classical or new age music from her collection.

After the shop's expansion was completed, Tina advertised in alternative newspapers and over the next several months developed a steady clientele. She set up appointments mainly for Tuesdays and Thursdays.

We had been together almost a year by then and felt we fit together well, and although I was feeling no heavy pressure, except for an occasional comment from my mom, I decided I wanted Tina to be my wife and the mother of our future kids. One of my old high school friends' family had a custom jewelry store and once while we were out window-shopping Tina had mentioned "I would love an emerald-cut stone, and a simple band of gold, if I ever found myself getting married. Hint, Hint."

I had listened to her, though at the time I just said, "That's nice to know. I'll pass it on to whoever the lucky guy is." I proposed on Valentine's Day at a small romantic French bistro I knew. The food was just okay but when her dessert came with her two-and-a -half carat diamond on top of her chocolate pastry, she was totally surprised.

She was without words for a few minutes but finally said, "Yes."

Tina wanted a June wedding, not too big, but family and friends certainly, plus employees. As usually happens, this small function turned into a major event. She had my mom and Helen to help her plan, plus Francis of course, but I for one will be glad when it is all over. For our honeymoon, Tina decided on California where she had always wanted to visit.

I had to make a few short trips, including one to Houston for market supplies again. Dan had just returned from Nepal. His descriptions and photos were amazing. He spoke of a small mountain valley high in the Himalayas. Pointing to a picture of snow-capped mountains he said, "They were less than a mile away from the place I had gone." Dan told of walking into the valley, first having to make a six-hour trek up the mountain just to get to the only entrance to the valley. "As I topped the ridge of the upper lip of the valley and looked down, I thought I had come to Shangri La, the fields of the rice in uniform rows of green plants, shimmering in the water. These fields were everywhere, terraced on different levels of ground. Deeper in the center of this green valley was an old Buddhist temple and grounds. The monks still work the fields along with the few families who still lived the agricultural life. I had come with a guide and three other adventurers. We stayed in the monastery that night and ate a very fresh vegetable soup with rice for dinner and a kind of rice gruel for the morning meal. The accommodations were sparse of course, but I had come for the views and a very special native hemp plant whose buds are used as medicine in Nepal, but about which the rest of the world knows very little. I had heard of its existence back in 1965 at a conference I attended where I met a guy who claimed to have smoked some." His description sounded more like a dream high; a feeling of euphoria, a rush of energy, senses heightened. You slow down and can go about your daily life. He called it "Spirit's Breath." Dan said, "I've also heard it called Mountain Spirit and a few dozen other names over the years, then whenever I encountered someone giving a description of, A High of High's, I'd always ask the person where it from is. The answer was always the same, "Somewhere up in the high mountains of the Himalayas in Nepal there grows this strain of marijuana."

Dan continued, "It took me years to finally track down this source. It is grown by monks and sold mostly to the shops and practitioners of the old healing arts throughout Asia. There is only so much grown each season and is rarely available in the U.S., even for people with deep pockets. I had to find it before I died, and when I got a lead last month, I booked the trip and guide. Max, the journey up there was strenuous, and I am not in the best shape but when we got to the valley the views alone were worth it. There were already over twenty other people from all over the world when we got there, even a few other Caucasians like me from Europe, or US, and Canada were there to buy. The bidding was in two-kilo lots, and it took me an hour to be able to bid on some of the recent harvest. Prices were steep even for me," Dan said. "I just kept waiting, letting the first lots go for what the market would bear, but as we got an hour into the bidding, there came a set of two lots, one after another, when most of the bidders were away for some reason, and I was able to buy them for less than $200 dollars an ounce. I paid $14,000 for 4.4 pounds of the most ideally perfect high I have ever experienced. There were several people trying to buy them from me even before we left to go back down that afternoon. All of us in my group which included a Chinese herbalist from Hong Kong, an Israeli scientist, and a rich California record producer who came for the "Hippy Hay," bought some buds, but most of them bought from resellers who were breaking the kilos down to smaller sellable amounts. Try this, Mr. Marijuana Man!"

Before me was the most beautifully wrapped holy smoke I had ever seen. The red rice paper joint looked too pretty to light, but when he did, all the previous words that were used to describe this buzz - euphoria, high, great feeling - fell short. It's like trying to describe the Grand Canyon to a blind person. You can use all the words in the dictionary you want, but you still fall short. You have to see it to experience it. This marijuana was like that, as Dan and I shared the next few hours, try as we might, neither of us could come up with a way to properly describe the feeling we were experiencing except to say, "Wow."

Since this was a rare product, not for just any consumer, he was selling this magic puff at $500 per 1/8 ounce to his customers. He felt if he sold some, then great, but if not, that was okay too; just more for him. The price of anything is based on supply and demand; the more the demand and the rarer the item, the price becomes what a buyer is willing to pay. This is basic Business 101. I worked on Dusty Dan all afternoon and got the price down to four ounces for $5,000. **"A friend in the market is better than gold in the chest."** It was only because I had made him deal years earlier on the Acapulco Gold that I was able to make this deal. Who knows when, or if, he would ever be back to the Himalayas? I spent almost $20,000 with him that day and would eventually get $45,000 back while still keeping two ounces of the "Spirit's Breath" and some ounces of the other high-end import just for my personal stash. Once the clothing market came, the cash flew and I had moved the entire primo products in less than two days. I could have moved a lot more of the mountain buds if I had wanted or had a larger supply. Tina and a few of our very select friends enjoyed the "wow" with us on rare special occasions. The supply lasted many years since it was used sparingly but always with great anticipation.

Earlier in the year I had been kicking around the idea of opening an unfinished furniture store where people could buy raw wooden pieces and stain or paint them themselves. From Little Oaks beginning, we were getting people coming in, who wished to buy more distressed pieces to sand or strip. I really did not want to inventory a bunch of someone else's junk and worried about finding it a home. But there was a demand, so I figured unfinished new pieces could give that do-it-yourself person a solid piece to start and they could creatively add their personal touches. I had been looking more seriously at the project just before we left for Europe. Now that we were back, I contacted a new furniture manufacturer who had a factory in South Carolina. The manufacturer's representative gave me some basic quotes and general information. Then as an afterthought. "Max, you know you might want to contact someone I know in your area, Fred MacGregor. His family had several stores of this type in Austin, San Antonio, and Houston. I had heard through the grapevine he might be looking for backers for an operation for the Dallas area, and it might work out for both of you."

I called Fred to talk to him about what I had in mind. "Max, his might work out for both of us; I know the business but am short on cash, while you have the lines of credit, so this could work. Why don't you come by my home tomorrow night, say eight, so we can discuss this more?" He gave me his address, and I was on time. I considered bringing a joint just in case, but on second thought, decided this was going to be business, not pleasure, leave the smoke for another time.

I had no sooner walked into this man's home, shook his hand and sat down when there was a loud voice accompanying an impatient pounding on the door. Seconds later, a flood of armed Dallas Police and DEA officers came barging through the front and back doors. At first, I thought they were after me, and I was going to be arrested for the

145 |

Houston slayings. I was so shocked I just sat there with my mouth open and felt all the blood drain from my face. "Hands behind your head, gentlemen," came out of the mouth of the policeman who was pointing his bright chrome gun at Fred and me. I was questioned about the kind of drugs I was here to buy. I pointed to the clipboard I had brought with me, my business card attached.

"Look, officer, I'm here about furniture. And that's all, certainly not drugs."

Fred was arrested for dealing after they found enough quantities of cocaine and amphetamines in the house to fulfill that requirement. It turned out that he had been out on bond from similar charges in Houston. I was arrested for attempting to buy drugs. Hell, I had only $37 in my pocket, and I had come in Tina's VW, so there was no cash stashed in the glove box. I was handcuffed and arrested anyway. At central booking I called Abe the attorney, who told me to keep quiet and he would see me soon. This business meeting cost me several thousand dollars and put me on the government's radar. My intuition had warned again about the joint, but another accident of being in the wrong place at the wrong time. I was questioned for over an hour but only said what I had in at Fred's house, and when I told them I had no more to say until my attorney arrived, they left me alone in a holding cell. They had no evidence; a person with only $37 in their pocket is not buying very many drugs. I had no record and was an established businessman, so I was not charged and was able to leave with my attorney. That was an expensive business meeting. I also had to pay to have Tina's car released from the police impound lot after the police had searched it. Thankfully, I am a stickler at keeping ashtrays clean of joints. One of the DEA people looked vaguely familiar, but I could not exactly place him.

Rule Number Two: (repeated and reworded) Develop and trust all your senses.

"The still small voice speaks to us but do we hear?"

During waking hours all of our body's senses, smells, heat, and cold. It also picks up sublevel signals that people do, tells. We pick up on as children it is second nature for children, but by the time we are adults we have so long forgotten how to use them that even if we were to get a warning, we ignore it.

This incident put me on notice and afterwards I had the feeling I was being followed on several occasions and that eyes were watching me. It may just have been paranoia, but I changed some of my habits. The house was continually kept clean of most products and smoking tools, papers, roach clips, bongs, etc.

I also decided to close that part of my business at least for this year, maybe forever. Tina was very happy with that decision and was now busy with her crew, planning for the upcoming wedding.

The big day in June came fast. Tina and I married at the Temple I had attended since childhood. My sister and her family came, as well as my brother and his current girlfriend. Tina's aunt came in, from Atlanta. I had several of my old friends there to share my day, though no Rodger. Tina, on the other hand, had a lot of her college girlfriends. Many of my mother's family attended and a few cousins, aunts and uncles from my father's side, plus the whole crew from both stores. The small wedding ended up twice as large as what we first planned, but I was told that was to be expected. The day came; it rained a little in the morning, but by the time of the ceremony, the sun was back out and the whole event was beautifully orchestrated by the planning community, who, of course, were very pleased with themselves. Tina looked like a model out of one of those bridal magazines scattered all through the house. I was just glad it was finally over. We left for California the next morning and our tail-wagging; four-legged child stayed with my folks.

We spent four days in LA visiting the standard spots; Disneyland, Universal Studios, the La Brea Tar Pits. We spent part of the day at Malibu beach watching people and took a bus tour of celebrity homes. I rented a car and we drove up Highway 1 to San Francisco for three days. We visited Fisherman's Wharf and Lombard Street, which is supposed to be one of the world's most crooked streets. Next, we visited one of my favorite areas, Muir Woods, which is across the Golden Gate Bridge. The giant redwoods there are some of the oldest living things on earth-over 2,200 years old and rising over 800 feet in the air. Some are as large as fifty feet in diameter which gives the park a mystical feel, especially if you have smoked "Spirit's Breath." The trees and ferns with small creeks running through gave me the feeling of comfort in a primitive world. We brought our lunch, had a great picnic, and just glowed in the moment. We were only hours away from the triangle, an area that grow's California's largest cash crop, marijuana and I'm thinking about expanding my import business and maybe coming back to Humboldt County to see if I might make a better deal here in the U.S .of A., when all of a sudden I hear Tina talking about my retirement from the, "game", as she calls it.

1976

Tangshan China 655,000 people die in an earthquake.

Viking 1 and 2 landed on Mars take samples and photos sending back information for the first time on the red planet. No life found yet.

The new $2.00 bill is issued, and it is about as popular as the expensive $1113.00 for a one -way ticket from New York to London on the Supersonic Concorde, which only took two and half hours.

America celebrates her Bicentennial: Johnny Cash is the Grand Marshall of the U.S. Bicentennial parade.

Even before the first of 1976 we began getting advertising salesman visiting both stores promoting the 1776/1976 old birthday theme. So nearly every merchant put a bicentennial twist on their marketing.

One particularly dreary afternoon in May, we were at the Little Oak, waiting for a let-up in the weather when an interesting older man with white hair and wrinkled, leathery skin walked into the store. He was smiling and appeared relaxed despite being wet from head to toe. I'm wondered, 'what do we have here?' He introduced himself as, "Buster Polinsky with Acme Publishing," but Buster was not just another advertising salesman as we were soon to find out. Mr. Polinsky had made an appointment with the previous occupier of this space six months ago, so he had not planned to see us. Buster was one of the best salesmen I ever met. Slow and smooth, he did not bring up his work, but rather spent the next hour entertaining Tina and me with several stories.

"I'm sixty-four, and I have been married four times, no kids of my own, but I've helped support five kids divided among my former wives. Yea and even after the divorces from their moms they are still my kids and I loved them." Yeah, I thought, I bet they find him easy shake-down for help or money. He looked like he was pushing seventy; A real road warrior. Buster had a rough, raspy voice from too many cigarettes, I guessed. "Ma'am, I have been a salesman since even before the war. I have sold, at one time or another, almost anything you could think of and many that you could not imagine."

Tina smiled and asked, "What are the unimaginable items?"

He grinned and said, "Legal or illegal?"

She laughed, coyly replying, "Illegal, of course."

"Well," he started, "I drove a truck in West Virginia when I was in my early teens. My kinfolk were all hard-working coal miners. When my dad gets drunk, he could be mean. I started to empty the alcohol dregs from his bottles after he had passed out. The collected liquid was cooked in the hills of the area, a white- lightening type of brew that I would hide. When I had collected enough, at least a gallon, from my dad, I would go out of town to make my deliveries. I could always find someone to buy my gallon of liquid fire." He continued, "After a couple of those sales, I was able to buy in larger quantities directly from some of the mountain folks. I was making more money selling moonshine than with the driving job, but the delivery job was a great cover. The Feds finally came in and busted most of the stills and arrested a bunch of people, luckily not me, but it ended one of my better money-making sales jobs. I still sell some illegal products, but they come in a different form." He then produced a joint out of his shirt pocket. "Would you like to share some?"

We went back to Tina's little workroom and smoked his offering which was not bad for a commercial-grade Mexican. I told him I had no need to purchase any but thanked him for the buzz. We spent several hours just passing the time and smoking. Before he left, we got around to discussing the advertising program he was selling. His idea was to run a sale on furnishings from 1776 or newer and sell my hanging baskets for $17.76. I liked the idea and ended up spending some money with him. I don't know if he gets all his customers stoned, but it sure worked for me.

Tina felt since she had been so busy with the wedding, she had not gotten to spend as much time with her friends as she had wanted to, so she decided we should throw a Fourth of July BBQ and invite many of the same people to our home. I was not into it, but I took a bit of advice my dad had given me on our wedding day. He had said, "Max, save your arguments for big battles and let Tina have most of whatever she wants." My mom and dad had been happily married for over forty years, so I figured he knew what he was talking about. Besides friends and family, Tina had invited the entire neighborhood association. Our place was to become the place to be on this Fourth. She had the celebration catered, ordering beef, goat, and chicken, and three kinds of potato salad, including her homemade basil special. She had fruit salad and a mixed bean salad, as well as smoked beans. She created a layered fruit and cake dessert in the shape of the 1776 American flag that looked too good to eat. I had cold drinks for the kids and beer or wine coolers for the adults. I discovered my wife was a very good party planner and hostess who always made people feel at home. Just before it got dark, we sauntered down the street to a park as a large group, where we were able to clearly watch the City of Dallas' fireworks launched from the Cotton Bowl at Fair Park. It was a great end to what had been a great day.

By the end of July, I started getting marijuana fever, but more importantly, Tina was also getting mysterious feelings that signaled she was pregnant. We were going to be parents, so I would not participate in that year's harvest. I did make several trips to see Dusty for my high-end clients and the market people, but I chose to call my regulars and explain I was not going to take orders this year.

Instead, we spent fall practicing breathing and the primal screaming and moaning which mostly came from me. Tina on the other hand, performed like a well-rehearsed professional?

1977

"Death does not knock on your door; he comes quietly when you are not looking."

*August 16, 1977 started out as just another hot Texas morning, but like most days, somewhere there were things occurring that would change many lives. This day would be one of those days. This day **the King of Rock and Roll** was found dead in his bathroom in Memphis. He was not the person who invented rock 'n' roll, or even the first to make it big in that genre, but he was the King and the steam behind that unstoppable train. We would find out later that, like other rockers had before him, Elvis died from an overdose of prescription drugs. For me Elvis had been my first connection to the music world, and though he was no John or Robert Kennedy, or Martin Luther King, he was important in his own way. He brought the races together in his music and he broke the color barrier at his concerts. He showed us that music is blind to the color of those who listen.*

Egypt's President Anwar al Sadat broke ranks with other Arab countries and recognizing Israel as a country.

Apple II computer goes on sale to the public.

The Trans Alaskan Oil Pipeline is opened.

Life settled into a predictable rut. As Tina's stomach grew, she started spending less and less time in the stores or with her massage clients, which meant I was spending more and more time in her place. We also decided it was time to look for our first home as we were a growing family. She and one of her friends, a realtor, began looking for new digs, and after a few weeks, had narrowed the search to two homes, each one different from the other. The first home was in a suburb of Dallas called Plano, in a brand-new housing development. We could pick out everything we wanted from the exterior style to the flooring, fixtures, appliances, fences, crown molding, the number of bedrooms and baths, one story or two, and the type of brick. This would be a total custom home to fit our dreams. It would also be the most expensive, so, of course, this was my mom's choice. The last home was an older home in our current neighborhood, built approximately forty years ago. It was a two-story English Tudor home with five bedrooms, one of which was set up to be a "nanny" room with a separate bath and small sitting room. This house had beautiful wood floors and woodwork throughout. The interior had custom work from the stair railings to the stained and beveled glass windows. The closets had built-in drawers for accessories and shoes; the interior doors rolled into the walls. Even though the kitchen needed to be modernized, the house had plenty of room and it felt so comfortable. The property had many old mature trees, and it was landscaped beautifully. The detached garage had an additional one-bedroom apartment above it. I felt at home the minute we walked in, and with a little work we would have a great house we could grow into. This was the house we chose, and Tina had the work on the kitchen done before we moved in. I also had the floors sanded and stained dark along with a few others that needed minor repairs.

Having our business and home in the historical Dallas neighborhood just added more to Tina's social status within her preservationist friends. Besides, she was now also a member of the Lakewood Professional Women's League, and a newly appointed member of the Temples Educational Committee. How she had time for all that was beyond me.

At least none of these groups were looking to blow anything up, or march for a cause, yet.

We moved in just a week before our baby was born on March 7, 1977. We spent fall and winter in Lamaze classes, learning to breathe and relax. Of course, it's easier to do in practice, I got the screaming and moaning down pretty good and when the actual event occurred Tina performed like a pro.

I wanted to call him, "Old," imagining his hand reaching out to introduce himself, "Hello, my name's "Old Gold, from Dallas, Texas." He was named after Tina's dad, Robert. I never thought I could love anyone as much as I loved Tina, but my love for Rob was all-consuming. I wanted so much for him and wanted to protect him and teach him; I guess all the things fathers want for their kids. People say your life changes after you have a baby, but I was not expecting how great the changes would be. The first six weeks were sleep-depriving nightmares, but by the second month's end, we had worked out a schedule for Rob and ourselves. I would cover taking care of Rob's feedings and changing his basic needs, from 4 a.m. to 9 a.m. and would help Tina when I was home. Tina had him early mornings and most of the rest of the day. She was breastfeeding so would use a breast pump during the day to store milk for my early morning feedings. I was fascinated watching her using the pump, and Tina was happy that I was so easily entertained. It was the nearest thing to sex that I was getting at the time. Rob grew so fast that he seemed to change right before our eyes every day, and I was a very happy and proud father.

I took the time when feeding him in the early morning hours to fantasize about what his life might be like. It dawned on me one morning; my dad had probably done the same with me, though I don't see Harold getting up in the early morning light to feed me. I had visions of Rob running the stores and then I saw my dad doing the same with me, so in a quick moment, I finally connected with my dad; my own dreams, for my own son, dreams mirroring my father's dream for his son, me.

I decided Rob could be who he wanted to be and work at what made him happy, hadn't I?

It was fast approaching the time when I had to make a decision to retire from dealing or feed my own addiction to action and money.

The lease on the warehouse was coming to an end soon. I had not used it for much except to store the trash pieces I did not want to fix or put in either store over the last few years. So I sold the contents to a hobbyist, and moved what little bit of papers from the old storage area.

I had only one more thing to do; call Rodger, who I had not seen in over a year, and let him know that I was moving, so he needed to get his spools and furniture along with his tools out of the warehouse by the end of the month. We had not spoken in 6 months but when last we spoke he seemed to be more interested in talking about coke and how much money he's making. I tried to give him some advice but he was not interested in hearing any of it. I still felt I owed him the call. When I left the only thing not taken was several thousand pounds of coffee beans in their burlap bags. I had always been a tea drinker, so I no longer needed the beans.

Throughout the summer and fall of 1978, I still was only dealing Dusty Dan's high- end product to my market guys. I missed the old business sometimes, but I loved my time with my son and family, so I was through with that part of my life, for good.

1978

The world population now reaches 4.4 billion people.

Bell Illinois introduces first cellular phone system.

Egypt and Israel sign a peace agreement at Camp David ending the Thirty-One-year war.

VW stops production of Beetle.

The Bee Gee's," Night Fever and Staying Alive "are burning the charts along with the Commodores' "Three times a Lady".

The movie "Deer Hunter" gives us a firsthand view of PTSD and if that was not thought provoking enough. "Close Encounter of the Third Kind," opened us to the thought again, that we may not be alone in this universe.

1979

China issues a one child per family policy.

USSR invades Afghanistan.

Three thousand radical Iranian Muslims students invade the US Embassy in Tehran and take ninety American hostages.

Michael Jackson first solo number one- album "Off the Wall" launches him to Super Star status.

Our daughter, Rachel Ann, was named after my grandmother and Tina's mom. She was born on February 14, 1979. While Rob was all boy, Rachel was to be a girly girl. Even from the beginning, she loved to be pampered, and a bubble bath was the highlight of her day. She could be very fussy if she did not get what she wanted, when she wanted it, especially feedings or a diaper change. It was as if she knew she deserved to be spoiled.

Tina had not hired any outside help when Rob was born, and when she went back to work, she, Wally and Rob all went to the store together, but when Rachel came into our lives that did not work out, it was too much with the dog and two kids. So, we went through the process of finding a nanny who was also willing to do some light housekeeping. Max was not quite ready for pre-school, and we knew filling the job was going to take a special person. That person came in the form of Miss Sula Martinez from Guatemala. She had just graduated from SMU. She had decided not to return to Guatemala as she had a boyfriend in Dallas who worked out of town during the week. She was looking for a Monday through Friday job that paid well but also provided room and board for the weekdays. Our house had been built for just this situation, with the nanny quarters just one bedroom down the hall from the kids' rooms. Sula loved children and had raised her own brothers and sister as a second mother when her mother had to go back to work to help support the family after Sula's father was killed during the country's political upheavals. Sula's degree was in early child education and the children took to her so well that we hired her right on the spot. She was a small lady with typical Hispanic dark hair and eyes. She had warm smile but told us she would not be easy on the kids and she would have them mind her. 'Good luck with that', I thought.

I cleaned out all of my personal stashes of smoke and moved them into the small apartment above the garage. The small one-bedroom was in pretty good shape, and I had already been using it as a getaway location when it got too noisy in the house.

Sula was a great nanny, though a little bit obsessive, as we would find out shortly after she started working for us. Tina came home one afternoon to find Rachel screaming as Sula was changing her diapers while wearing large yellow rubber gloves. It seemed Sula was a germ freak and the baby was terrified by the yellow gloves. At least I knew I did not have to worry if the house was clean with Sula around. The dirt, dust and germs did not have a chance to settle. She was a bit eccentric at times, but she also introduced us to some of her native dishes which included potato and spinach soup and pumpkin pancakes. The children loved her, and she did a great job working with Rob on his Sesame Street skills and teaching him Spanish as well as improving his English vocabulary. She would play trucks and build blocks with Rob to improve his motor and hand-eye skills. Sula was slowly breaking Rachel of "Me, me, me…Now, now, now" behavior for which we were both very thankful for. We had Friday nights, all day Saturday, and Sunday to ourselves as a family, and we did not expect Sula to help during the weekday evenings when we were home. All in all, it was a great situation for all of u

When May of 1979 arrived, I started getting the old marijuana itch. I had stayed away for most of four years and had been lying low. By all outward appearances I was just a normal businessman. Everything was going smoothly, but life was predictable and almost lulling me to sleep in boredom.

I was to find a different market than the one I left. The items that Dusty had been bringing in for years were now the items everyone wanted. Dan and I talked about it as we smoked some Colombian Red, he had just gotten in. "Max it's beginning to get harder and more expensive to get the little bit I get in. Cartels and street gangs have taken over from planting to distribution. Columbians and Jamaicans are here in Houston in a big way, and they are retailing what I use to have exclusivity on. "

"Do you know any of the players here?" I asked

"I met a few Jamaicans when they first came to town, lively group but in business they want to sell their product like it was 24 KT. Gold no room for me to make any money. And they don't have any time to waste, because the Ruthless Colombians are coming in and forcefully taking over old territories and they are taking no prisoners. I have done my best to avoid them all together. "

The products from exotic world ports were what some of the people wanted, but my business sense knew not everyone can afford the high dollar high. For most of the brotherhood smoking; Street weed, Skunk-weed, or just get you high Mexican, that always got the job done, was what they could afford and wanted.

So, against Tina's wishes and ill feelings, I made a trip to Mexico to look up Alejandro and Jorge. I did not find Alejandro, but I did find Jorge, that late afternoon, in one of his fields. He greeted me like a long-lost son. We talked of the old days, and I showed him pictures of my kids like any proud father would. He had eight kids from three different mothers. I had asked about Alejandro, but in a very short reply, I was told he no longer worked for him, so I let the subject drop. I would later find out from one of the field hands that Alejandro had tried to force Jorge to retire, but that had backfired. No one had seen or heard from him since. Jorge said, "I have most fields under contract, but for you I am sure we can put some product together." It seemed a lot of the Columbian Cartel was now heavily invested in Mexican drugs. Besides their own cocaine, they wanted marijuana and the growing poppy businesses. "Do you want any of the white powders?" he asked. "Many of my other buyers are adding these items to their list and are getting rich," he smiled.

"No, I'm only interested in one product, but what about the high-end Colombian Red or Gold?" He just laughed.

"Do you want one pound of that or one Kilo of mine, that's how much they are getting for their pretty plants?"

"Thanks," I replied." He seemed to understand. Fresh product would be available as usual in late August or early September. "Jorge is there any way to cull through the fields and cut the male plants down before they flowered and pollinated the female plants.

His reply, "I have one location where it might be possible. It is up in a valley in the mountains but will be more expensive due to the extra labor and the trucking expense to bring it down to a convenient loading location." We spent time coming up with an agreeable price and worked out the logistics.

As I traveled toward the border, I came to the conclusion that Jorge had probably already culled the male plants at that location to grow a better grade of marijuana. He could not do this at the other fields because, even if he had done so, the field around this would still have male plants and some of the pollen would find the female plants. I was paying a lot more than I expected but knew from the past that I would be able to sell a higher grade of product for more.

On my way home, I stopped by McAllen and called on Lee Daniel. "Max my business is growing almost too fast. I have six-chromed out new Kenworth's out on the road now. My oldest son is also working with me and the two of us have all the cargo capacity you'll need." Of course, his prices had also gone up from four years ago. His claim the federal government was really cracking down, and everything was tightening up.

After I left Lee's shop, I stopped at a truck stop and made several calls to old customers to see if there was any interest in the new, improved high-end product, and guess what, I was received with warm greetings and most of the group was still around minus a few who had been busted. I also got the names of a couple of new buyers who might be interested in talking. When I called one, he said he had heard of the famous "MM." My reputation preceded me. I got a sinking feeling when I talked to him, so I never called him back. By the time I got home, I had most of the details worked out except where I was going to store the inventory safely, but I had an idea in the back of my mind.

Tim was an original member of my **Brotherhood of Smoke** group, from back in 66. He was now teaching at a small college, and we stayed in touch over the years. He was one of the people who I could share a good smoke with. He appreciated the product. Tim lived on a 100-acre farm about an hour from Dallas. The house sat way off the road out of sight, along with several outbuildings. The roads up to the property were good, all-weather rock roads, as were the roads throughout the farm. There were a few truck farmers and over-the-road truck drivers who lived in the area, so a big road truck and trailer coming down the road would not receive undue attention. Tina and I had spent several weekends visiting him and his wife, Lorie, over the years. We really enjoyed the fresh air and laid-back country living. Tim loved to hear some of my stories. He never asked to buy anything from me, since he grew his own. He did, however, always enjoy my samples when we got together. But what Tim really liked was that I always brought him some seeds of various unique exotics or seeds from good old, nasty weed.

Tim had a spot down near one of his stock tanks where he grew his large organic garden of vegetables, a one-acre orchard of fruit trees and a forest of pecans, but it was on the other side of the orchards, over the hill and through the woods to his personal garden. Here, away from madding crowds, growing in harmony, were his personal plants. It was like visiting Marijuana Land. He must have had thirty different types of plants each growing differently. He was a "Maven of Pot," and like Dan, he liked variety. He never wanted to sell the fruit of his labors but would trade.

Tim knew I dealt some pot but had no idea how much I was actually buying and selling. He had one barn large enough for a tractor-trailer to back into. It also has a concrete shop floor which would be the perfect place to store my product. I just had to find a way to entice him.

I called Tim shortly after I got back from Mexico, "Tim I have a proposition for ya." We agreed to meet one afternoon that week for lunch when I would explain my ideas to him. "Look Tim, there will be only three deliveries by road truck, and besides the driver, only you, Lorie and I will know the location. I will be coming and going for a few months, but I'll call you ahead of time, to give you guys a heads up, and we'll work around your schedule."

"Max I am intrigued, and you say the money for the storage will be in cash. I tell you what; I'll discuss this with his Lorie and get back to you." He called back asking, "When do I need the area cleaned up for you?" I had my new storage facility. The barns were filled with hay, so the smell wouldn't be a problem. He rarely had visitors and those that did come had never gone into the locked shop, which made it the perfect spot. I only had to wait for the harvest.

In the early fall of 1979, the north Texas area had a lot of rain, and I began worrying about the truck getting stuck on the road to the farm and barn. But Tim had added rock to his road. By the time the first load was there, I had all the equipment waiting, a loading ramp and a pallet jack set for fast emptying and stacking. The night of the first delivery, Tim had made sure his wife Lorie and kids were away, just in case. I liked the way he thought. It took just a little over an hour; I thought our first transfer went very smoothly. We were smoking the new green before ten. I had brought my own trailer to take a load up to Oklahoma. I was on the way to Oklahoma before 11 p.m. The 1979-1980 season was open.

The whole- years' worth of work went well, except for two small hitches. One came when I got to an agreed drop-off site. The buyer started arguing / bargaining about the price, giving me a hard time. This, of course, was not the first time this thing had happened, but it always made things awkward. I asked him to pick a brick, open it, roll a joint and then tell me it was too expensive. After only two hits he agreed it was good pot, but he only had enough cash for so many pounds, and he wanted the rest on credit. "You have two choices," I said. "One, get what you can pay for now or two, buy nothing. That is, it because I am out of here in just a minute." He bought what he could pay for, and I sold the rest he couldn't buy at my next stop. The second problem came when I called my Bossier City customer. He had always been a good buyer and never had a problem with the price as long as the product was top quality. His girlfriend answered the phone as she had been expecting my call. It seemed he had been busted on drug distribution charges and was in jail, but she knew his customers. If I could front the product, she could pay me back fast. I explained, "Look it would not do either of us any good for you to start dealing with your old man already under the microscope." That was an easy call. Again, my timing was perfect. If I had made that delivery a few weeks earlier, I could have been caught up in the investigation and been busted. Timing /luck is everything. **"There is nothing more successful than a lucky man."**

Most of my clients were more than happy with the year's harvest, and I could have sold twice as much if I had had it. I was gone most weekends from September through November and one weekend in December

I was experiencing a bit more heat from one person and it was not positive encouragement, and cold in other ways, a reminder of how truly un- happy she was. My reasoning was, "this was me, and it was the same me I was when she met me, married me and agreed to have children with me."

We were at a stale mate. So, she put her time, energy and efforts into the kids, the stores, and the growing list of groups she was working with or for. I took care of everything else and paid for it all.

1980

"God created a world full of many little worlds."

May 18, 1980 at 8:32 a.m. local time, in the state of Washington, Mount St. Helen erupted, producing a record lateral blast on the northern flank of the volcano, sending lightning bolts thousands of meters into the air and flattening millions of mature Douglas Fir trees covering over 600 square kilometers in a fan-shaped pattern. In seconds, the eruption killed fifty-seven people and sent ash all over the area and into the air which would cover the earth for days, changing weather conditions.

The New Year, 1980, came with much joy and happiness at my house. All my family was healthy. My businesses were all doing well, and I had lots of cash put away. Who could ask for anything more? We had developed a Sunday ritual at my house. During the winter, after breakfast, the whole family would gather in the living room where I had the fireplace going. I would read the funny pages from the newspaper to them. Rachel was almost one and just liked hearing my voice and her brother's laughter. I would read in various voices and always add dialogue to each comic. The kids would play on the floor or sit in my lap. Tina would often finish reading the paper while I was doing my reading-aloud stint. I look forward to this time each week.

One Sunday, an advertisement for a new Gunite swimming pool "for as low as $4,995" caught Tina's attention. "Look," she said as she pointed the ad out to me. "We could have our own swimming pool for less than $5,000."

Upon closer inspection of the ad, I noted on the bottom of the ad in very small letters, "Electric, decking and permits not included." "Here's the gimmick. When you add the not-included items and increase the size of the pool from a 14' x 28' size, to a reasonably sized pool, you are now talking about over $20,000, plus landscaping and the cost of upkeep," I countered. "Besides, the kids are really young right now."

I saw the look of determination on Tina's face, and I knew this was going to be a fight I was going to lose even before it got started. "We could just call and see, couldn't we?" she asked.

"Sure, go ahead," I replied, knowing in my gut that this whole thing was not going to be a good choice on many levels.

"Just think, the kids can swim every day and what about all the family fun times we will have?" Tina was already sold and thinking of the future, while I was thinking of all the extra work that was going to be my responsibility, plus the added expense.

We had a large backyard with many old mature trees. Some of them would need to come out, and though the yard had a five-foot chain link fence surrounding the yard, it too would have to be replaced with a solid eight- foot wood privacy fence. I would also find out that all my utility cables ran through or over the yard, and they would need to be moved. Of course, we would need a spa so we could use the water in the winter. The one thing I would regret the most was losing the mature trees and space. Max loved driving his motorized dump truck around the yard chasing Wally or helping me collect the dog poop. Max would drive the truck, and I would load the droppings in the dump truck's bed. He loved the idea of helping me though sometimes he would drive off before I could load the truck up, and I would have to chase him down.

All in all, Tina had three different pool companies out to give us their ideas and bids. Each guy would take at least three hours going over measurements, talking about pool layout, design and all the exclusive features that only their company offered. They all drew pools and decking ideas and when they got to the end of the presentation, they tried to get us to sign a contract. I had to threaten one guy just to get him to leave. All of them would put car salesmen to shame. In the end, all the quotes were very close to each other and after doing some research and calling references. We ended up picking one that a club member had referred to her.

They were to begin in February and to be done in six weeks; they actually finished in the last week of May. The final cost was $22,350, not too far off from my original Sunday morning 'guestimate'. I also know that it did not add $22k to the value of our home, but my wife and kids were happy along with all my neighbors who would soon be using it.

I went to Mexico to work my deal out with Jorge for this year's crop, and he introduced me to another of his sons, Carlos. The young man had become Jorge's number one man, and I would be working with him in the future. There was something about Carlos' demeanor that put me off. I'm not sure if it was his hooded, reptile-looking eyes or just his abrupt mannerisms, but I had to deal with the man, so I did my best to work with him. Jorge had always been warm and friendly, but there was nothing but coolness coming from his son. After concluding our deal, I asked, "Is it alright if I come back later in the summer to visit the fields?"

It was something I had done before, but his reply was a prompt, "I would rather you not. But if you must, call first." The whole mood of the deal seemed to change, and I had a forlorn feeling that this year's deal was going to be a problem.

Back in Dallas, life had a new pattern. With the pool done, I found myself spending more time entertaining family and friends, mostly Tina's but a few of mine too, and the neighbors who always seemed to be over with their kids. I was the one having to deal with the chemical issues because more kids meant more pee and poop in the pool. My dreaded thoughts of pool ownership were coming true, and I could only hope that as the novelty of the pool wore off, we would have our lives back. The stores were doing well, and I was still sending someone to Europe at least once a year. The real bargains were beginning to dry up, and we found ourselves going deeper into the rural areas to find the deals we really wanted. I personally did not like these old cities of Europe, so most often I would send Helen or Francis. Sometimes I would use a buyer's service, but normally I did not like what I would end up with, so I usually only dealt with reliable dealers with whom I had developed a relationship and who knew what I liked and what would make me happy.

Tina hired a lady named Linda Dugan, to work the Little Nut, full time. Tina was working at her massage business more and more. The store was not covered as well as it should. I did not like to have to call the big store to get someone to cover. In walked Linda on one of those days when I needed to be in several different places at once while Tina was busy with clients. All of the other store staff were busy also. Linda reminded me of Lenora Evergreen, Dusty Dan's rich friend from Houston. She was in her early 50's, with the same big hair. Recently divorced, she was raising two teens by herself. Her husband had run off with a younger woman, and she had actually come into the store to see if we would be interested in buying some of her excess furniture since she was soon going to have to downsize from her large Highland Park home. She was a very classy lady, dressed well and had good taste. Just as she was finishing her story we were getting to the point of her visit. Tina finished with her client and joined us. She recognized a person in need and offered Linda a cup of tea. The two of them talked while I worked with a walk-in customer. By the time I was done with my customer, Tina had figured the situation out. "Look, Max, Linda needs a job so she can keep her house and the kids can stay in their old school. I am going to hire her to help in the store." As it turned out, Linda was socially connected with a lot of our high-end clients and could bring in even more of her friends as customers plus she knew many of Tina's new friends at the preservation league.

When I called Carlos to arrange a visit in late July, he was his usual abrupt self. "It's not convenient for me now. Just call back in early September and we'll work out the pickup schedule," he said and hung up the phone before I could even say anything in response. I got the feeling I was about to be screwed. When I called back during the last week of August, I had already gotten the transportation set with Lee and his son. When I finally reached Carlos after three attempts, he told me, "Your man was down here last week and picked up over half of the harvest."

I yelled, "What man? I don't have a man. I have never had a man!" My anger was getting the best of me, and I knew I was not going to get my contracted product. He was either going to sell it to someone else for more money or something funny was going on. It took all of my self-control to maintain some form of composure and not go totally ballistic. He said a guy in his late thirties with reddish-blond hair with big white teeth came down pulling a trailer and said that you had sent him to pick up half the load. He'd described Rodger. He told me that they were not really ready for us, but Rodger insisted and paid for 6,500 pounds. It hit me a like a wet slap on the face. When I had cleaned out the warehouse, I had a box of papers and receipts from when I was flying the pot out myself, and it looked like someone had gone through them. At the time it hadn't meant anything; now it made sense. Rodger must have gone through the papers, done some basic math and figured out the general area I was flying to. He just drove around the area until he hit the right person who could point him to Jorge, then to Carlos. Carlos said there were only about 3,000 pounds left of my contracted plot. He could probably get me some more commercial grade product, but of course, it would be the same price as what I had agreed to pay for the other pot. I was mad and screwed, and there was nothing I could do but smile and take it. My 6th sense is rarely wrong, but still, I cannot always do something to protect myself, especially when I don't know what's coming.

I drove straight to Denton, went to Rodger's house and found it was empty. When I finally reached his mother, she told me they had been fighting and she had not seen him in over six months, but it was an off-hand remark that pulled the whole story together. She told me that the fight was over his new business partner and his slutty sister, who was from New York and had been leading Rodger around by his nose and she did not like him; she called him *"Vinny, the sleaze ball."* I thanked her. Now the whole thing made sense. Rodger could have never pulled this deal together, let alone have gotten that much money scraped up for the purchase. Vincent Gambo was behind this rip-off. Carlos probably knew I had not sent Rodger but figured it was an easy way to squeeze more money out of the tonnage without lifting a finger. I don't know if Jorge knew of the incident, but I was sure he would know before I got there, and Carlos was not going to get to keep the extra cash if I had anything to do with it. I flew down to Mexico the next day. Jorge picked me up at the landing spot and he, Carlos and I met over lunch to calmly discuss the ordeal. Jorge was old school, so he did not like the way things went down. He was a man of honor, and we had always been square with each other. That there was no call to him or to me told him that Carlos had actually known of the rip-off. When he finally got the truth out of Carlos, the pot that he sold Vinny was actually only commercial grade. My stuff was just being harvested and dried as we spoke. Any time large sums of money are at stake, there are people around who will do what they can to take it from you. Carlos got caught. I do not know what, if anything, was going to happen to him, but I received my order and would not have to deal with Carlos in the future, at least as long as the old man was still in charge. I really never felt I got the truth. It could have been the way Carlos told it, or Jorge may have been in on the deal and just wanted to see what I was going to do, but he did not want to lose me as a customer, so he made Carlos a heavy. The three truck loads came to the farm uneventfully; for that, I was grateful. I was followed and inspected when I flew back from Mexico and landed in the U.S. But I was not carrying anything; as far as they were concerned, I had gone down there just to buy fruit.

I never saw or heard from Rodger ever again though I eventually found out what happened to him. Many months later, my sister Judy had shipped a box of hand-me-down clothes for Rachel. Kids generally outgrow clothes before they are worn-out; so much of what was sent was nearly new. Judy had used newspaper to pack in the open space in the box. I was making our first-of-the-season Sunday fire, crumpling that newspaper to light the fire when something in print caught my eye. I unfolded the wadded- up paper and read a story from the Annapolis News. One Rodger Sampson from Denton, Texas, was arrested on the 301 following a standard stop for a traffic violation. When the officer approached the car, he detected a strong odor of marijuana. Upon further investigation, the trunk was found to contain over twenty pounds of high-grade marijuana along with a suitcase holding over $100,000 in cash. It is amazing how when you ask the universe a question, you sometimes get a reply in an unexpected way. I became more vigilant, not knowing for sure how desperate Rodger had become, if he would stand up, or make a deal with the law to cut the time of his sentence.

Rodger and I had been like two peas in the same pod. His betrayal cut me to my basic principles. This was worse than the blood bath in the pasture in spring. He was just thinking with his cock, not his heart, which he seemed to have lost. I still cannot believe it after all these years. It's still a broken bone of contention and has weight upon my heart. The betrayal for what, short-term physical pleasure and small-time gain over a twenty-five plus year friendship. His betrayal is something I probably will never get over.

I sold my product that year differently, for some of the clients seemed to be short on cash, or the price increase allowed them to buy only in smaller quantities at a time. Many had put more of their working capital into other drugs. At any rate, I had to make more trips back and forth to sell the tonnage. It was the end of March before I sold the last of that year's harvest and even though I made a good bit of money, I was beginning to think it was not worth the risk. This year's headaches and the extra road time had really taken a lot out of me, and it was no longer fun and exciting. Maybe this will be my last year, I thought.

1981

"The workman's rights always take precedence over those of his employer."

"To work for another man is often like taking honey from a bee: accompanied by a sting."

Poland, the Solidarity Labor Movement holds a general strike across the country causing a work shutdown. The Polish Communist government responded by imposing martial law. The workers of Poland, as a group, resisted and overthrew the government, bringing in democracy for their people.

The United States Federal Air Traffic Controllers went on strike. Though they were union workers, they worked for the federal government. President Ronald Reagan did not want the nation's airports to close down. After a short warning President Reagan fired the striking controllers and brought in military personnel to do the job until new people could be hired and trained.

As a small business owner, I viewed my employees like they were family. Occasionally, problems arose, but nothing that could not be worked out with a little conversation or money. Over the last few years, Tina and I had started buying some investment items. I had been buying gold coins all along for emergencies and long-term growth. These I kept in a safe hidden in my garage. We also bought artwork which I did not know a lot about, but with the help of my mom and Helen, we made some good purchases. Tina fell in love with the works of artist John Singer Sargent. She particularly loved his paintings of children. I liked Andrew Wyeth's work, and for color, we bought a few Chagall's and a beautiful Kandinsky. I also bought Tina some gold jewelry; some with and some without stones. I purchased a gold Rolex diamond watch for her and an old 18k Patek Philippe watch for myself. For a weekend retreat we bought a lake house that was an hour away. On one side of my garage at home I stored the 1946 Mercury Sportsman Woody Convertible I had acquired in a swap for product. She took my heart away at first sight. The deep dark blue exterior with mahogany side panels and is trimmed with honey oak. The chrome was brighter than any Christmas tree tinsel. The rich leather interior spoke old- world craftsmanship. *"Just sitting still, it looked like class,"* is what Tina would say. We took her out for parades that Tina signed us up for and the kids just loved "Old Blue." We would also use it on weekends when the weather was right. On a rare occasion when he was not too busy, Rob would help me wash or wax Old Blue, and there were times we both enjoyed ourselves after we dried off from the water fights.

We traveled more as a family to Hawaii and skied at Steamboat Springs, Colorado. We also took the kids and my folks to Disney World in Florida. We felt relaxed in our lives. In the spring we got a shock. My dad had a heart attack. Fortunately, it turned out to be very mild, but he was 69 years old and it had given the whole family a scare. It made us all aware of how fast life circumstances can change, not always for the best. My mom wanted him to sell the appliance store and retire, but he compromised by cutting back his hours at the store and promoting one of his employees to operations manager to run the day-to-day functions. He still had a place to go every day, but he did not have to open and close the store. If he did not want to, he did not have to show up at all.

I had already made arrangements last year for this year's planting and despite all the problems of last year, I decided that since my furniture business was slowing down due to the economy, and I needed the security of a sure thing with my marijuana business, I would continue as usual. The demand for pot increased and no matter what the price, all I ever got was a couple of moans but never a reply of, "It's too high! I don't want it."

Much of the population was now snorting mountains of cocaine, and there was always a news story on the TV or in News Papers about a large cocaine bust here or there. South Florida was experiencing lots of deaths by bludgeoning, chain sawing and of course just by the old fashion way by numerous pieces of lead entering their bodies, and these were standard news items. Then the stories of drug lords like Pablo Escobar who had ordered the killings of politicians, or the blowing up of buildings of competitors back home in Colombia was a monthly on- going story.

Cocaine was a product that was making some people very, very rich but pot had its own market which overlapped with some consumers. My customers were always interested in what I sold no matter what other Drug was the in thing. I had many who were interested in only being members of the "Brotherhood of the Smoke" exclusively.

When I went down to Mexico in the beginning of September 1981, things were a mess. The U.S. federal government had sprayed defoliants on several of Carlos' fields. Thankfully, my plot was in the hard-to-find mountain areas in more dangerous airspace for an aircraft to maneuver. Old man Jorge had moved more of his growing operation into these areas. By doing so he could get a better price and was more secure in several ways. He let Carlos handle the open field operations, which at this time were forcing Carlos to harvest what he could and clean up the mess to replant. I was glad I was not buying his poisoned pot. No telling what damage smoking this weed would cause to someone's body. Carlos was too busy to give me any real grief as I worked with Jorge on these loads. The first load was delivered on the back of a bobtail truck at the loading area we had been using over the last few years. The driver backed up to the side door of Lee's trailer and I spot-weighed the bricks as they were being loaded into the trailer. The whole loading, weighing and sampling took less than two hours. Both Lee and his son came down on the next trip, but Lee made the last trip alone. Each time the process got easier and quicker; the loading and unloading at Tim's farm got simpler.

Fall of 1981 went sweetly. I had fewer small buyers who were purchasing only twenty-five to fifty-pound quantities, and for the most part, I found these buyers always ready with cash in hand. This year's crop was one of the best I had seen in a long time; the buds were beautiful, medium green, but very long, over fourteen inches each for the most part. I had my regulars like Sonny and Rudy in San Antonio and his brother in Austin. I made two trips to Shreveport Louisiana, Oklahoma City and Tulsa, Oklahoma and one trip each to Fayetteville, Arkansas, St. Louis, Missouri, and Kansas City, Kansas. An once again made a trip to Amarillo, to meet Evan Burk, my Scottsdale client, at the midway point. I also brought with me an old player piano that he had shown interest in. It took both of us and a wino off the street to unload it out of my trailer and into the back of Evan's rented truck. He was planning to make it a main drawing piece in a theme bar he was about to open in a few months.

1982

The beginning of 1982 found the economy in a severe recession,
  The price of gasoline is ninety- one cents a gallon.
  ATT&T is ordered to break up into 7 independent Baby Bell's.
  Seven hundred thousand human protesters gather in Central Park in New City and protest the proliferation of nuclear weapons.
  Musically Paul and Stevie had "Ebony and Ivory". Steve Miller's "Abracadabra" is facing the new contender Michael Jacksons' and his second solo album, "Thriller".

By late March I had all but two hundred pounds sold. Since I had not received any money for the piano yet, and Evan was willing to give me a check for the pot and the piano which would help to put some needed money back into the store. I flew it out to him. I rented the plane at a North Dallas private airport and filed my flight destination papers for Phoenix, but I first flew to a small grass strip near the farm and met Tim with the last of our year's harvest. I was loaded and back in the air in less than fifteen minutes. My trip out to Arizona was long and uneventful; I landed at the golf course as usual, and we loaded the remaining product in his truck.

I left early the next morning to head back to Dallas in the rental plane, but I kept getting the feeling that I was being followed although I could not see anyone. It was one of those feelings I get every now and then. The hairs on the back of my neck stood up and I had a sick queasy feeling in the pit of my stomach like nerves of apprehension for something I could not put my finger on. When I landed at the private Addison Airport in north Dallas, I was greeted by several dark-suited, official-looking guys. One was a now familiar face, Officer Dwight Longstead. He took me into an office and questioned me, while the DEA and FBI thoroughly inspected the plane. Most drugs come from Arizona, not from Texas to Arizona, so they had assumed I was bringing the drugs *in*. They found the large check in my briefcase but there was also the receipt for the delivered piano. They kept asking me questions. My only statement, "If I need a lawyer, I want to call mine now. I have nothing else to say." but in the end, they had nothing on me so they had to let me go.

This was a warning to me, **Strike one**. The next few months I felt the heat and it seemed I was being watched and followed. It did not bother me because I was not doing anything to bring attention to myself or anything illegal, but I did get a notice from the IRS of a business audit as well as a personal audit. I was not worried because I had always been a stickler for keeping records and making sure my taxes were paid fully and on time. The audit, though a pain in the ass, went well and I even got some tax money back after it was all said and done. Tina's and my personal taxes were scrutinized thoroughly and after a couple of face-to-face meetings with our accountant and us, we ended up owing them a few thousand dollars because they disallowed a couple of deductions. I think they did this to see if they could trace where the fine money would come from. Luckily, I had some savings.

I should have walked away from the business, right then and there, but it was an addiction, and a challenge to see what I could get away with right under the noses of the authorities. It might have been the rush or just stupid greed, but whatever it was, I was irrational.

The purchasing, loading and unloading of this year's tonnage went as smoothly as I could have asked for. I was careful and took evasive routes when I made my deliveries and double-checked all my security precautions. I did not take on any new clients and actually dropped a few who I had done business with before as I sense trouble as I talked to them on the phone. I did not make sales to Evan for both of our sakes, and he seemed to understand that after I had put him on the DEA's radar, it was best for both of us. The regulars actually took more this year, so I had fewer trips and made more money than ever before. Next, my Tulsa buyer decided he wanted to change the meeting place. When I got there, I started getting my gut warning as I approached the street on which the house was located and the hairs on my neck and arms stood up. I noticed a van with dark windows parked several doors down from the house, so I drove past the house and found another car with four guys sitting inside on the other side of the street. I just kept driving. I headed back to the highway and then pulled off the road to wait and see if I was being followed. Sure enough, a few minutes later, the same car with the four men drove past heading for the highway I had planned to use. I decided that this load was not going back to Dallas, but instead, I headed toward Arkansas to one of my clients who always had cash and who I was going to see next week anyway. I made a week of it traveling back roads to buy some furniture and decorator items for the stores. When I got home and was unloading the trailer at the warehouse, I swore I was being watched. **Strike two**. I had just slipped by on that deal.

Despite the grim economic news, I decided as a spring break bonus, to take the entire staff of both stores, and the green house crew, along with my brother, sister and their families and my folks on a four-day cruise that left Galveston Island and went to Cancun, Mexico and back. The sunshine and sandy beaches were just what we all needed to recharge.

On the trip, Linda Duggan's son, Freddy, who had been working part-time for me while he went to school, approached me one morning on the deck. "Mister Gold," he said, "do you have a few minutes to listen to a deal I want to propose to you?"

"Sure," I said. "What do you have on your mind?"

"Well sir," he said. "I need to borrow $10,000 to buy some stuff that I can sell in just a few days. I can pay you back quickly and make us both a good return."

"All education starts with forbidding" I smiled and replied, "Freddy since you have not mentioned what you are buying and because you know that whatever it is will sell very fast, I have to assume it is probably illegal, and I personally do not need to get involved in that type of activity, no matter what it pays. What I recommend is that you stay away from such deals as well because, sooner or later, you will get burned. Spend your time and energy thinking about how to make money legally. Now if you have a legitimate idea, come back to me with full details. Then we'll look at it more closely, okay?" He went away shaking his head, and I didn't know if he really absorbed what I had just advised him. This brought back a conversation my father had with me on a plane trip home from Mexico more than a decade earlier. I hoped he had listened better to the same advice my dad gave me, than I did.

I wrote a check from the company account for some of the trip and had paid cash to the travel agent under the table. I really had to watch what I did with my cash now that I had both the IRS and the DEA looking over my shoulders.

I was sure 1982 was going to be a great year. Tina and I had even talked about having another baby, but Tina wanted to put it off for a while since she was just getting her own body back in shape and was really enjoying working at the little store and with her massage clients and her committee work. Each year seemed to go by faster and faster. It seemed like only yesterday that Max was a small child and Rachael was a newborn. Now Max was almost five and so full of himself, and my baby girl would soon be three. She walked, talked and was daddy's little girl, at least for a little while longer.

When late spring came, I made my trip down to Mexico and met with Carlos, as Jorge was not feeling well. "Due to a scheduling problem your load will not be ready until late September," Carlos told me. "And don't be calling Jorge; he is not involved in the business anymore." I was not happy. It would put me several weeks behind, but I knew there wasn't a lot I could do about it. Carlos was not going to negotiate with me. He just smiled with his lizard-like face and walked out of the bar where we had met. He loved to show his power and flaunt it. I never could figure out why.

The summer started and our backyard again became the neighborhood meeting ground for all the young kids and their parents, and any artist, writer or expert on some subject or other that is currently interested Tina. The stores were doing only so-so, and I actually had considered closing the Little Nut. It was hardly making its payroll and expenses didn't leave a lot of profit, but Tina loved the store, and it was close to the house.

One night in late August, a story appeared on the national news about a South Texas trucking company. Three of its trucks stopped at two different entry points, crossing back into Texas from Mexico. In the front of each truck trailer were secret compartments. Two were full of illegal drugs, cocaine and marijuana. The third truck had twenty illegal migrant workers. When the camera focused on one of the trucks, sure enough, it was Lee Daniel Trucking. It seemed I was being forced into making a critical decision; find a new importation source or walk away. I was lucky I did not have $500,000 worth of paid-for products confiscated by the government. I decided that night I had had a good run, but all the signs were pointing to my calling it quits once and for all. I made a few calls and let it be known that I was out of the supply business.

That fall I was antsy, but I managed to stay busy. I even went to an auction in London to bid on a few specialty pieces that I wanted in the store's show room. I was only gone four days, but a good four days to be gone. It turned out Freddy had not taken my advice and had somehow scraped enough money together to buy cocaine. When I got home, I was confronted with the problem because he had been busted and Linda was beside herself. I had to worry about the authorities trying to get Freddy to roll over on me by offering him a plea if they could connect us together. Tina had contacted our lawyer Abe and had Linda meet with him. He went to work on Freddy's case. I called him too when I got back, "Abe I'm concerned Freddy being a part-time employee of mine that I might be brought this mess even if I am not involved."

He said, "I'll check things out and get back to you ASAP". The police had stopped Freddy's partner and found a half-smoked joint in the kid's ashtray. Upon closer inspection of the car, they found the cocaine in the car's glove box and the partner had rolled over on Freddy as the mastermind. When Abe called back, he said, "MA, I do not think there is going to be any problem getting the charges dropped. Freddy did not have the drugs on him, and the other kid comes from a well-to-do family with the right political connections to make the whole thing go away. And no, I don't think the connection between Freddy and you had ever come up during the interrogation."

1983

The Chinese population hits 1 billion people.

12 million Americans are unemployed, the largest number since before 1941.

Gasoline is $1.25 per gallon.

5000 United States Marines invade the Island nation of Granada to over throw the recently installed communist government who took power by force with the help of Cuban train forces. The Marines save the 1000 US students and citizens living on the Island from the red threat.

Motorola Corporation releases the first Mobil phone.

The New Year 1983 came and went. I was reevaluating the idea of an unfinished furniture store again. I also shopped for locations and found two I liked and had suppliers located for pine and oak furniture. I had contacted a couple of high-end furniture manufacturers to find out about buying unfinished pieces from them.

In late April, just before I had made up my mind to go ahead with the project, I was contacted at the house by someone I did not know. They said they were friends of Billy Williams, my broom corn farmer friend. I asked for their phone number and told them I would call them back in a few minutes. I went to a pay phone and tried to contact Billy but had no luck, so I made my call back to the caller who said his name was Richard. He told me he had grown a crop, but he was not able to move all he had harvested and had eight hundred pounds left that he would sell cheap, $25,000 cash. My gut said no, but my itch said yes. I could flip this with just one call and delivery. I would have the money to open both locations. I agreed to meet him at a rental storage place in Durant, Oklahoma, at the Oklahoma-Texas border. I continued to call Billy but never could reach him, so I brought my truck, trailer, cash, and scale.

I arrived at the meeting site early as usual. The place seemed unusually quiet, but it was a weekday, so I didn't give it much significance. I was not getting a positive vibe but passed it off to doing business with an unknown person. Richard showed up in an old Dodge truck and we talked for a few minutes. "I really appreciate you helping me with this," he said.

Then he opened the gates to the facility, and I followed him onto the property. There were four rows of buildings with units on both sides, each 10 x 15. I followed him to his storage space. As he got out of his truck, I could have sworn I saw a slight smirk cross his face. He opened the locked door and rolled it up. Inside were fifty- pound marijuana bales, just like Billy had delivered to me before. It didn't take us long to weigh a few bales, load my truck and exchange the cash. I was already spending my profits from this deal in my mind; which location would open first. Then out of the blue, a feeling of an icy chill covered my whole

185 |

being. I looked around. No wind. The next few minutes were a blur. I had no sooner gotten back into my truck and started it when I looked up to see Richard motioning to me. I rolled down the window to see what he wanted. He bounded over, this time it was to arrest me. He pulled out a big automatic pistol, pointed at me, and he said, "Max Gold you are under arrest, please get out of the truck and put your hands behind your back." Moments later, a black and white police car pulled in front of me to block my escape. Two armed officers spilled out, drawing down on me at the same time. Then an unmarked black car pulled up. From this car emerged my smiling nemesis, Dwight Longstead. In a very precise yet forceful voice Longstead said, "Max Gold, you are under arrest for interstate trafficking in an illegal controlled substance." It had become a federal crime once I crossed into Oklahoma. He read my Miranda rights. "You have the right to remain silent…," he said. I followed this advice except to request to make a phone call to my attorney. This was not the first time I had been confronted by Longstead, but these circumstances were more consequential.

I was so angry at myself I could hardly breathe, and yet I was also worried what all the negative publicity would bring to my folks and my wife and kids. They did not deserve the attention that would come from this and that made me feel even worse.

I was busted in a reverse sting, attempting to buy illegal drugs. DEA Officer Longstead had been on my tail for almost fifteen years and had come close to busting me several times, but I always seemed to have second sight and slipped out of his snare. Not this time. I called my Black Suit Abe Blend from the Bryan County Jail, and as we had planned, I said nothing until he arrived the next day. "Max from I see they got you dead to rights, you are pretty well screwed. On the other hand, if you cooperated with the DEA and help them bust your clients, I can work a better deal to get a lighter sentence."

"Abe, I screwed up, no one else, the deed is mine alone, and I'm not going to involve anyone else in this."

"Ok, then I'll work the best deal, I can for you." I was also being charged with cocaine importation. As they had no evidence, my attorney was able to get that dropped because they had no evidence and though the police and DEA came to my home and businesses, they could not find anything there to bust me for. I lost my beautiful Merc convertible, the lake house. My antique gold watch, and all the cash I had stashed in several bank safety deposit boxes, along with a few paintings. All of these items had been paid for in cash or at least partially in cash, so I could not prove where the cash had come from. Luckily, my business was not affected. I had been smart in keeping things separate and had proof of income for my home, and the big stores' buildings.

Tina had been expecting such a call from my lawyer for years, so when it finally came, it was almost a relief for her. She knew it was over except for the punishment. If it had not been for my wife's strength, I don't know what I would have done. I had lost over 2.5 million in cash and other assets plus what I would owe my attorney. Things could have been worse; they never found my safe with the gold coins and a little cash that Tina would need to keep things afloat for the next few years.

The publicity was not great for my family or for the businesses as I had dreaded, but my family all stuck with me. At the very short trial, I pleaded guilty. Life went back to semi-normal for them. After their shock the staff seemed to weather through as well. We had to close the Little Nut, and though the sale of furniture and plants slowed down, Tina was able to step up and keep things running. People have short memories, and there are always people who can afford finer things at a reasonable price.

Abe had gotten me the best deal he could, three and a half to seven years, depending on me and if could keep myself out of trouble. This was a federal crime, thankfully, not a state of Texas or Oklahoma crime where the prison systems are understaffed and underfunded, very dangerous residences for a lightweight like me. My new home wasn't too far from my family, so they could visit.

That buy had been my **third strike**; no one's luck runs forever. Mine had run over seventeen years until I broke two of my cardinal rules —*Know your customer*, doing business with someone I didn't know and couldn't verify**. Two, the most important, I had ignored my gut feelings.**

Every single day since the bust, I ask myself why I had taken such a stupid risk. Why did I ignore my own rules? For that matter, why was I never satisfied with what I already had? I have finally come to the conclusion. It really doesn't matter why or even what I have done in the past. It is the past. I cannot change it, but I must deal with what is in front of me and the new life that awaits me.

"For am I not a Jew-28% fear 2% sugar and 70% Chutzpa"

ZADYISM

Zadyism is a piece of knowledge distributed verbally with love, and an insightful knowledge of life. Some of these bits of knowledge are original, but most are borrowed/stolen from someone else. Though, Zady never claimed any of these thoughts as his own, "just good words."

What you don't see with your eyes, don't invent with your mouth. Old Jewish proverb Page 2

A Jew is 28% *fear*, 2% *sugar* and 70% *chutzpah*. Old Yiddish saying Page 2

Experience is what we call the *accumulation of our mistakes*. Oscar Wilde: "Experience is merely the name we give our mistakes." Page 2

"If opportunity does not knock, build a door." Milton Berle Page 12

God watches over fools. Otto Von Bismarck: "God has a special providence for fools, drunkards, and the United States of America." Page 17

"The best lessons in life can be the ones we learn from someone else's mistakes." Zady Page 24

If you give a pig a chair, next he will want to dance on the table. Old Yiddish saying Page 35

"Be prepared." The Motto of Boy Scouts of America page 39

"To achieve great things, two things are needed; a plan, and not quite enough time." Anne Frank Page 61

"He who has the gold, Rules." Jean Rousseau Page 63

Even a blind squirrel can find a nut every once in a while. Old Appalachian saying Page 76

There is no proxy in transgression. Talmud Page 79

The door of success is marked 'push' and 'pull'. Achieving success is knowing when to do what. Coco Chanel Page 84

"If you don't want fleas, don't sleep with dogs." Ben Franklin: If you lie down with dogs you get fleas. Page 121

If you do the crime, you do the time. Hip expression used in 60's-70's, taken from TV show Barretta, which Motto was, "Don't do the crime if you can't do the time." Page 131

Beware of your friends, not your enemies. Bible Page 131

"If you swim against the current, you cannot stop ,you can either go forward or back." Chavat Yair Page 137

A friend in the market is better than gold in the chest. M. Maimonides Page 140

"Death does not knock on your door; he comes quietly when you are not looking." Zady Page 147

"There is nothing more successful than a lucky man." Zady Page 158

God created a world full of many little worlds. Old Yiddish proverb Page 159

The workman's rights always take precedence over those of his employer. Talmud Page 166

To work for another man is often like taking honey from a bee: accompanied by a sting. Torah Page 166

"All education starts with forbidding." A. Einstein Page 172

THE BUSINESS RULES

The rules developed over the years to conduct business with the least amount of risk to me.

Rule Number One: A nail that sticks out is just looking to be hammered. Don't stick out. Old Japanese proverb: The nail that sticks out gets hammered. Page 24

Rule Number Two: Trust your gut. Rule Number Two: God speaks in still small voices...so listen. The Bible. Page 24

Rule Number Three: Cast no stone into a well that gives you water. Don't do business at home or keep inventory there. The Bible: Cast no stone in to the well from which thou has drawn water. Page 31

Rule Number Four: Know as much as you can about each of your customers. Common sense Page 35

Rule Number Five: Sell what you know, or know what you sell. Zady Page 37

Rule Number Six: He who wishes to be wise should study monetary laws. Talmud Page 38

Rule Number Seven: Draw from the past, live in the present, work for the future. Theo Herzl Page 40

Rule Number Eight: When opportunity arrives at your door, offer him a chair. Old Yiddish saying. Page 47

Rule Number Nine: Experience is merely the name we give mistakes. Oscar Wilde, "Experience is merely the name men give to their mistakes." Page 83

Rule Number Two: (repeated and reworded) Develop and trust all your senses. The still small voice speaks to us but do we hear? The Bible.

THE AUTHOR

STEVE KRAVETZ's narrative talents grew from practicing the art of oral storytelling. The author developed his storytelling skills as a sales tool during his over fifty years in sales. It did not matter if he was selling men's clothing or steel beam, swimming pools or cars, "Prospective buyers always became relaxed and attentive when I told a story or two." Steve's first public recognition carne in 1993 when he won first place in The Texas Champion Liar Contest at the State Fair of Texas. This seventy-year-old widow from Rockwall, Texas, can currently be seen performing stand-up storytelling at various venues throughout the Dallas Metroplex.

www.ingramcontent.com/pod-product-compliance
Lightning Source LLC
Chambersburg PA
CBHW020612120726
47905CB00003B/760